. . . The outlaws gathered together a short distance away, waiting impatiently for Margarita as she looked fixedly upon the passenger who stood stock-still, glowering defiantly.

"Do you want to kiss me, too, desperado?" The strong voice challenged Margarita. The lady looked fearlessly into Margarita's black eyes.

Undisturbed by her words, Margarita thought: You owe me, foolish Anglo. And I will collect every peso of it before I am through. She looked at the rest of this group cowering before her, fearing for their worthless lives, and waited for the anticipated rage to grip her as it always did after a robbery. As it did, she felt gratified.

She glanced for a final time upon the lady who had the courage of the angry bull smoldering in her eyes. Surprisingly, Margarita felt no vehemence within her soul toward the beautiful traveler as she did for the others. Perhaps it was the woman's bold spirit. Disturbed by the softening in her, Margarita whispered fiercely, "Bah!" and kicked roweled spurs into the sides of her horse.

To my sisters Mickey and Pat

And to Karen

Yellowthroat

by Penny Hayes

The Naiad Press, Inc.
1988

Copyright © 1988 by Penny Hayes

Printed in the United States of America
First Edition

Edited by Katherine V. Forrest
Cover design by The Women's Graphic Center
Typesetting by Sandi Stancil

Library of Congress Cataloging-in-Publication Data

Hayes, Penny, 1940—
    Yellowthroat / by Penny Hayes.
        p.   cm.
    ISBN 0-941483-10-X
    I. Title.
PS3558.A835Y4   1988   87-35203
                                                         CIP

Chapter One

Margarita Sanchez endured the jostling of the mud-wagon with strained patience, motion-sick and longing to be anywhere but a prisoner of its interior. The wagon's six passengers, shoulder to shoulder, knee to knee within the box-like structure, their feet propped up uncomfortably on the overflow of lumpy canvas bags of printed matter and express packages from the rear boot, sweated profusely.

With the heavy downpour of this morning, the stock tender at the last swing station had harnessed six mules to the vehicle, a light weight canvas-topped coach that could handle the worst of roads, even one thick with mud like this road. Those continuing further north would not ride the heavier and more comfortable Concord stage again until the roads were dried out by the sun and beaten relatively firm by wide-rimmed wheels. But coach travel, whatever its conditions, would not be troubling Margarita much longer. The next station, now only a few miles away, would be her last coach stop.

Margarita Sanchez was considered by some to be a handsome woman; by herself, plain. Of medium height, she was slender and strong, trimmed down to bone and muscle from the past two years of Spartan living and hard riding. Black shiny hair, pulled tightly behind her ears into a bun, surrounded an oval face with smooth skin of olive cast. Whenever she laughed or was angered, her dark eyes flashed with sparkling clarity; her sooty lashes and eyebrows accented their penetrating look. A thin nose was almost too long but a feature that she liked about herself. Full lips, now pressed tightly together, concealed even white teeth. The blue satin dress she wore rustled slightly as she crossed her legs in an attempt to relieve tired knees held too long in one position.

She closed her eyes against the glare of the bright afternoon sun and started to rest her head against the back of the hot leather seat, but the brim of her small blue bonnet interfered. She removed the hat, placing it in her lap, then once again closed her eyes and leaned back. Absently she reached up and rubbed a slender finger against a slight scar which split the hairs through the center of her right eyebrow, the small disfigurement the result of a fall as a youngster against a metal bucket. As a child she had rubbed the itching wound as it healed, and now the gesture was old habit. She licked her lips and

2

teeth and then nearly bit her tongue as the mud-wagon hit a deep pot hole, jolting all the passengers into full wakefulness. The travelers exchanged impatient mutterings before again settling down.

Trying not to disturb the woman next to her, Margarita readjusted her position slightly to lean more comfortably against the wagon's side. Glad this leg of her journey was almost over, she gazed at the rocky terrain, at prickly pear cactus dominating the landscape. Soon she would be able to saddle up and ride in unbound freedom back to the meadow nestled within the Sangre de Cristo Mountains, yet another week's ride from the swing station where her horse was stabled and her gear stored. She could have continued further north by coach, but a saddle suited her better. Besides, whenever going home to Carizaillo, in old Mexico, she must never appear at her mother's house on horseback.

Unlike returning to the meadow, the trip to Carizaillo to visit her family was never as tiring nor as long. She was unfailingly filled with anticipation and excitement as she conjured up thoughts of her mother's face lighting up, her brothers and sisters gathering tightly around her to watch wide-eyed and silent as she pulled from her purse American paper dollars and gold and silver coins. The coins would be passed reverently from hand to hand to be fingered and fondled and bitten into for authenticity. Her mother would say again, "You should not give away your money, Margarita. You will need it to start over." And Margarita would answer as always, "I have plenty. The ranch brought in plenty when I sold it." And again she would cringe inside at the lie.

After the early death of her father, her brave and generous husband had sent money to her family. Margarita had many times thanked God that Seth

3

Merrill's horse had needed water that day on his way to Saucillo to buy cattle. Her mother had fed him and her father had talked for hours across the table to him about cattle and horses, speaking in broken English; Seth had responded in passable Spanish. It was clear that Seth only half listened to her father's monologue; he was casting longing eyes toward Margarita. He had stopped several more times in her village after that, and within the year he and Margarita had married, had bought two thousand acres of land in New Mexico, had begun their own ranch.

This time in Mexico, Margarita had spent two weeks with her family, bursting with pride as she helped her mother and sisters buy whatever food they wanted and needed, and new clothes and shoes. She had been able to shut out thoughts of her own dark life, behaving just as any woman might who was still unmarried and living at home, helping with the cooking and cleaning and the raising of the little ones.

The wagon came within sight of the swing station, bringing Margarita back to the present. Groans of grateful relief came from within the stage as it rolled to a stop. The passengers stiffly disembarked and stretched their cramped legs.

Margarita stood aside waiting for the stock tender to exchange teams. In fifteen minutes the mud-wagon was again on its way, without her, its passengers once more captives of their cramped cabin on wheels.

"I'll want my horse now, Tom," she said to the tender.

Tom had been at the station as long as Margarita had been traveling through, occasionally passing an hour talking with her while she delayed her ride north. He had learned to accept the strange behavior of the lady who was brave enough to ride alone. He had been a big help to her from time to time, carelessly revealing information

4

about the stage line. Today, however, she wished to be on her way immediately.

She headed inside the long, low adobe building the station master and stock tender called home, to change into riding clothes. Wearing black pants, a white shirt, and heavy black boots and spurs, Margarita exited the building, carrying saddlebags stuffed with her finery and hard tack in one hand, her coat and wide-brimmed hat in the other.

"Gonna eat some vittles before you go?" Tom asked.

"You call that smelly old salt pork and corn dodgers vittles, Tom, and I'm going to shoot you for lying to me."

He laughed and held the reins of her big stallion as she lashed the bags and coat to the rear of the saddle. She paid him with a gold coin then took the reins and mounted up. Donning her hat she gently spurred the horse forward, her mind already calculating how much money she thought she and her friends might take from the next group of Anglos, the job now only two weeks away. An almost pleasurable hatred flowed through her veins.

It had been Anglos that night who had wantonly killed her husband and stolen all that she and Seth had built together. She vowed that as many of the wretched dogs as possible would pay for what they had done. To do that she would rob them at every opportunity, and kill them if necessary, to replace what they had taken. Man or woman, it did not matter. With deep satisfaction she would continue to take their treasures from their shaking fingers. They would cringe beneath her threatening pistol.

She kicked her mount into a lope. The meadow suddenly seemed more like home than home, and too far away.

Chapter Two

High on the driver's seat, the stagecoach's guard sat slumped forward across a Winchester .44, its threat cut off by a bullet through the man's right side. The driver of the coach held his arms high in the air, the reins of the six-horse team still clutched in his hands, looking like carelessly strung telegraph wire.

Inside the stage sat four men and a woman. "My God," uttered one of the men. His lips were white, his face gaunt as he mopped sweat from his neck and brow. The others averted their eyes from the pallid stranger who, like the rest, had regretfully elected to take the early morning stage to Santa Fe.

The rising sun reflected dully off the barrels of the four masked bandits' pistols. They held their skittish horses in check while a single outlaw jumped from his stallion and pulled open the door of the coach with a vicious yank.

"Get out," he commanded gruffly, and gestured at the travelers with a careless flip of his wrist and a curt motion of his gun.

Each passenger obediently exited, then stood silently beside the stage. While the bandit hastily searched them with rough hands.

"Hurry up," snapped another gunman to the rummaging bandit. His big horse pranced restlessly beneath him making it difficult to keep a steady barrel on the victims.

"Shut up," Margarita whispered harshly. She knew the wisdom of saying as little as possible. Someone might later recognize their voices — her voice — and discover a major clue to this band's identity. After all, how many women were outlaws? Only Belle Starr over in the Oklahoma Indian Territory. Since that put Starr too far east to be a suspect, the law would be looking for another woman, and Margarita sure as hell didn't want them looking for her. And if she had to keep her mouth shut, then the boys damn well better do the same.

The man plundering the passengers had purposely waited to search his final victim. The woman stood unflinchingly as he deliberately mauled her, soiling her dress, his large calloused hands sliding over her shoulders, across her breasts, and down her thighs. Even though she had remained quiet, as had the other travelers, she had not shown the fear that they had. Forced to turn over the money she had hidden in the cleavage of full breasts, she unbuttoned the front of her dress with a steady hand as the highwayman eyed her lustfully.

She slapped the small roll of bills into the palm of his rough hand and hissed, "Bastard!"

Laughing carelessly, he stuffed the money into a cloth sack.

She spat into his face.

Unexpectedly humiliated before the others, the thief loudly cursed the woman, forgetting Margarita's early warning to keep his mouth shut. His hands full of booty, he clumsily grabbed his victim, and kissed her roughly on the mouth through his dirty, stained bandanna.

A sharp blow across his head brought the bandit to his senses. A rider spoke quickly and with sharp command. "Cut the team loose. Then mount up. We're finished here."

Without argument the robber turned to obey, holstering his sidearm and drawing a large knife from a boot sheath to slash the straps from the horses. Margarita rode near the woman to see that she was all right.

Never before had she felt an iota of concern over a cursed Anglo. Except for Seth, she had never before seen one who had displayed such bravery. She hated to admit it, but the courageous lady was to be admired.

Of medium height and slender build, the American woman was graceful in movement, even in her agitated state. The only visible evidence of her unease were the long, thin fingers playing nervously against the sides of her plain brown dress and the dusty blue eyes, above prominent cheekbones, that flashed angrily at her tormenters. Unlike most western ladies who hid behind parasols and sunbonnets against northern New Mexico's pounding summer sun, she was lightly tanned, the color

8

lending her face a healthy glow. Shiny blonde hair, whitened by the sun at the temple, was worn parted in the middle and wound about her head in thick glossy braids and adorned with a small white hat decorated with a simple plume. She was tall and slender and stood with severe pride before Margarita. With deliberate motion, she carefully rebuttoned her dress.

The men of the gang scattered the team far and wide, slapping ropes and sweat-stained hats against their thighs to get the big animals moving. Dust billowed up behind the frightened horses in their efforts to escape the charging men. The outlaws gathered together a short distance away, waiting impatiently for Margarita as she looked fixedly upon the passenger who stood stock-still, glowering defiantly.

"Do you want to kiss me, too, desperado?" The strong voice challenged Margarita. The lady looked fearlessly into Margarita's black eyes.

Undisturbed by her words, Margarita thought: You owe me, foolish Anglo. And I will collect every peso of it before I am through. She looked at the rest of this group cowering before her, fearing for their worthless lives, and waited for the anticipated rage to grip her as it always did after a robbery. As it did, she felt gratified.

She glanced for a final time upon the lady who had the courage of the angry bull smoldering in her eyes. Surprisingly, Margarita felt no vehemence within her soul toward the beautiful traveler as she did for the others. Perhaps it was the woman's bold spirit. Disturbed by the softening in her, Margarita whispered fiercely, "Bah!" and kicked roweled spurs into the sides of her horse.

Heading directly northwest for the Sangre de Cristo Mountains, the bandits rode rapidly over the hill they had

9

earlier descended to take the stage by surprise, and in seconds were out of sight.

In another hour it would be dark. Already stars were beginning to twinkle in the clear early evening sky. The wind was unusually warm tonight, almost hot, and the dust from the horses' thundering hooves pounding the dry earth rose into the air, sticking to the outlaws' sweating skin.

Margarita ignored the grit that flew into her eyes, the grime that scratched the back of her neck beneath the dirty, red bandanna worn loosely about her throat. Her hat, tied with a rawhide thong around her neck, flew behind her, freeing hair that had been worn carefully tucked out of sight during the holdup. More dust and dirt clung to a heavy, loose-fitting coat worn over a white long-sleeved cotton shirt. The dust worked methodically into every crease and fold of her heavy black pants. Calf-high boots worn over the pants trapped uncomfortable heat within, swelling the feet that had worn them for so many endless hours. But soon she and the others would be safe; soon she could shed these filthy clothes and rest. She rubbed a finger across the scar in her eyebrow and felt the grit on her skin.

Through the seat of her pants and the insides of her legs, she felt Billy Black give an added burst of strength on this long hard ride back to the hideaway as the jet black courses drew nearer and nearer to home. He laid back his ears as she spoke to him, and she reached forward to give the powerful stallion an encouraging firm pat on his sleek neck, dark and foamy with sweat.

For the past two days, they had traveled northwest as fast as possible, resting only during the hottest part of each day, climbing ever higher into the mountains through the Sangre de Cristo's steep foothills, threading their way through dense forests of pine, fir, and spruce thick enough to conceal cold, clear lakes and bubbling trout streams, and where elk, deer, bear, and mountain lions roamed freely. The mountains towered above them, ever beckoning to the tired outlaws as they drew nearer and nearer to home.

Almost to their final destination now, the riders pulled to a slow trot as they reached the bedrock of Carrico Creek that twisted and turned through the hills. Having reached this part of the stream, they knew their tracks would be lost to lawmen and bounty hunters. They traveled up the creek's center for a mile where the bed lay clean and free of soil or loose stones and pebbles, leaving no telltale signs floating downstream indicating their direction of travel.

They left the creek fifteen minutes later, cutting directly west to Lost River Canyon where ice cold water ran forcefully between steep walls of rock, some walls a few hundred feet high and others more than a thousand. The powerful torrent began miles above where the bandits entered, then continued south from there, to meet the Conchas River.

For the next twenty minutes the outlaws wound their way upward over an ancient and narrow trail along the river's edge as water roared through the gorge sending welcomed droplets of deliciously cool spray and mist over their sweating bodies. They came to a widened area where a tall thick growth of sturdy shrubs grew along the length of the canyon for a half mile or so. Midway in the brush, they rode directly into it and in seconds completely disappeared from sight.

Margarita remembered back to just a little over two years ago, to their initial entry into the narrow refuge they now entered. That day, as they waited for the posse to catch up to them, they had all been ready to die rather than be taken alive. The four outlaws had huddled together like cornered animals, hidden behind the bushes, sixguns drawn, hammers back, ready to blast away the very moment that the posse made its way around the bend in the creek. But by sheer chance, only moments before the posse would reach them, one of the men had spotted a hole behind the brush. A rapid inspection showed it to be wide enough for a horse and rider to enter, and one by one the bandits had ridden single file into the opening, the final bandit carefully brushing away their telltale tracks. Once inside, they found that the hole opened into a canyon. As they continued to ride deeper and deeper into it, the posse had passed right on by, continuing to follow the old trail, never suspecting what had happened to their prey.

Safe within the walls of the steep canyon once more, Margarita could finally relax as she and the others continued their upward journey. No longer did she feel the need to frequently glance over her shoulder as she had when they first discovered this escape. No longer did she expect to feel at any moment the impact of a bullet knock her from the saddle. This was a secure place, a place she trusted would never be found.

As the outlaws followed the increasingly wider crack, the earth rose higher and higher until the trail gradually opened out into an uncommonly large, grassy meadow concealed from the valley below by pines and cedars growing along its steep edge, creating a natural fence.

It was an unusual spot, well protected by its position, but no so high itself as to be barren. At two thousand feet it was rocky to be sure, but the plentiful sweet clover and surprisingly dense grass was belly-high, making it possible to pasture stock here. More pine and cedar grew thick and tall against and up the mountainside behind the meadow until, hundreds of feet above, the trees petered out, turning into scrubs, windblown and poor.

Since the meadow's discovery, the men and Margarita had worked like mules to bring in supplies and materials, always under cover of darkness. From the cedars they had cut enough logs to construct two crude cabins and a horse shed. They had steered a stream down to the foot of the pasture, building a large rock cistern to capture the sweet water. Fences were not needed for there was no way to come or go except by the single trail leading into the meadow, and that way was blocked by a simple gate to prevent a grazing horse from wandering down the path.

This permanent camp was a place to which they could flee during good weather and in which they could winter safely, and there had been few complaints during their heavy labors.

In the darkness, the group dismounted stiffly before the horse shed, moaning and grumbling to themselves. Margarita lit a lantern as the others automatically began to unsaddle their tired mounts. She removed her own richly carved and heavily silvered saddle, and then silently she and the men rubbed down each animal before turning it loose to rejoin the rest of the herd to roll and scratch the thick dust from its hide.

Their brief chores complete, they gathered together in the larger of the two cabins to divide their stolen goods.

A crude table and three cots, each with a small chest at its foot, nearly filled the single-room dwelling. Several shelves nailed to the walls held metal plates and utensils, tins of food, lanterns, dry goods, and dark bottles of whiskey that gleamed in the cabin's frugal light. Against the back wall was a stone fireplace set into the packed dirt floor.

In the gloom Margarita sank with a groan onto one of the cots as the men sat themselves down heavily around the table, on hand hewn, three-legged stools. By the light of a lantern placed near one edge of the table, the booty was spilled noisily from the sack. One by one, the men began to inspect each piece of jewelry.

"Come on over, Margarita," invited Bert. "Count the money."

Reluctantly she rose and joined them. With little enthusiasm, she split the bills and change equally, and in turn, was handed what was considered to be a fair share of the jewelry.

"Sam, gimme that bottle." Bert Simson, the tallest of the men, spoke with quiet authority as the loot was passed around, his piercing brown eyes half hidden by a sombrero seldom removed. He was dirty and bearded, his mouth a mere slit beneath an overly large nose. Heavy dark clothes, smelling strongly of sweat and horses, hung on his scrawny frame. He was a man to be feared, but he was fair if those he dealt with were fair. If he believed they were not, he shot them dead with the well-oiled gun he wore on his hip.

Sam Abelson reached for a bottle from the shelf behind his head and passed it across the table to Bert. Sam could have fooled the devil himself with his believable lies and angelic features. His full lips continuously played with a smile, and women read things in his deep blue eyes that he didn't mean at all. A slender man, ordinarily clean shaven, with rosy cheeks setting off wavy black hair, Sam was full of charm and impeccably clean in person. He was an expert rider and the group's bronc buster; his reflexes were lightning quick. The wanted posters throughout the territory verified it along with several men who had learned too late to be around to testify to the fact. He cared for only two people, he once told Margarita: her, and a wife waiting for him in Mexico, somewhere, whom Margarita resembled.

"Time to get drunk," he muttered to no one in particular, and took a second bottle from the shelf, pulling long and hard on it and then belching with deep contentment.

Margarita ignored his coarseness and turned to watch Bill Bleu take a long pull on yet another bottle, his Adam's apple rhythmically bobbing up and down beneath a thin and scraggly beard. His stringy hair was long and greasy, and his clothes stinking, not having been changed in months. A runt of a man, with exceptionally bowed legs which drew him even closer to the ground, Bill resented his body and had brawled throughout his younger life to prove he was as much boy as any of them. When he grew older, he proved he was as much man by robbing and killing. He was the meanest of the bandits, and Margarita had once seen him shoot a good horse just because the animal had stung his face with the swish of its tail as he had walked by.

"Have a drink, Margarita," he offered generously.

"No thanks," she answered curtly and stood to go. She wanted nothing on this earth from him.

He grabbed her by the wrist and yanked her onto his lap. "I insist." Smiling grotesquely, he thrust the bottle close to her face, almost gagging her with his breath and the sight of his teeth rotted nearly to the gums.

She slapped him with a hard stinging blow. Harder than usual because she so frequently went through this rubbish with him and tonight she was just too tired to

15

argue. Once again he was mauling her and none of the others would lift a finger to stop him. "You're an animal, Bill," she snarled as she wrestled from his grasp. "A pig!" She snatched up her share of the loot from the table and jammed it into her pants pockets.

Bill threw back his head and laughed rakishly as she tossed a string of Spanish insults at him, and at the others who would not help her.

"What the hell were you doing at that stagecoach?" Bill demanded belligerently. "Why didn't you ride when the rest of us were ready? You could'a got us all shot."

So that was what was making him such a fiend tonight! It had been her delay as she paused to study the courageous lady with the blue eyes that was setting him off now. "I wanted to look at a brave Anglo for a change," she retorted with a saucy toss of her head. "I haven't seen one in years."

Mimicking her heavy Mexican accent, Bill parroted, "I haven't seen one in years," then cursed her soundly in English.

"*Puerco!*" she flashed at him over her shoulder and angrily left the hut. She went to her own cabin, a lodging as rough hewn as the men's, muttering obscenities at Bill all the way. She emptied her pockets onto a small table before lying down on the single narrow cot. Like the mens' dwelling, this one's two small windows and open doorway were left uncovered during the summer months in spite of cool nights. She enjoyed watching the rising moon's bright light cast silvery shadows over the barren earth floor, across the table and its only stool, onto well-stocked shelves. Against one wall and built of stone was a cold fireplace. At the foot of her cot, she too had a chest in which she stored her personal effects and a few women's garments.

16

She felt the soft rays of the lunar body calm her. She wanted food, but was too exhausted from the two days' mad dash back to the meadow to eat. A posse never failed to track them as soon as someone at the holdup site was able to ride like hell for help, and this most recent job had sapped her energy — as each one always did. But she didn't care. Her wealth was growing. In another couple of years she would recover all she had lost — if her luck held out. In two years at the most, she would leave this despicable lot of Anglos forever. Had she been able to find Mexicans, she would have ridden with them, but she was in northern New Mexico Territory, where there were fewer dishonest Mexicans than dishonest Anglos.

Loma Parda, over on the Mora River crawled with gambling, "Taos Lightning," and loose women, and so she had ridden to the town to find those she needed and knew would be there. Fortunately, the nearby soldiers from Fort Union bothered no one except the Indians, and there were few of those wandering around anymore since the signing of the treaty in '68. She had given thanks on more than one occasion to Kit Carson, the man who had played a major role in getting the treaty signed, whenever she rode alone on her reconnaissance through New Mexico's expansive territory.

Money talked very loudly at Loma Parda, and after some checking around the town she had been able to find a small but promising band from among its questionable citizens. The men had listened closely while she laid out her plan. She would be the 'point' and act as the group's scout. Who would ever be clever enough to suspect a beautiful señorita of *espiar* while strolling the streets of first this town and then that, as she cunningly gathered information for a possible holdup? The men had liked the bold idea and right away had begun their felonious work.

Occasionally Margarita found it necessary to use her charms to learn what she needed to know; but she had never failed at her task.

Fearful they might one day drive her away, the men generally left her alone except for occasional harassment. And if things began to get out of hand, Sam came to her aid. The men had soon learned that a band with a woman, unusual though it was, worked well, and their pockets were kept relatively filled. No one really wanted to foul things up.

Margarita rested on her cot for awhile, then rose and walked out into moonlight brilliant enough to reveal the trail that wound up the side of the cliff just behind her quarters. She took soap with her, and a towel and fresh clothing.

She climbed the path through fragrant pine trees for fifteen minutes before coming to a stream which broke into a large, clear pool of water trapped by huge rocks and boulders. The pool was surrounded by trees and shrubbery, but Margarita had little doubt that she bathed without privacy, at least during daylight hours.

She dropped her dusty clothing at her feet, too tired to give a damn if the whole world was watching right now, and slipped into the cold water to swim to the deeper area of the pool. She dove to the bottom, let her breath out slowly until she thought her lungs would burst, then swam quickly to the top, breaking through the water's black surface and gasping for breath. She ducked again and shook her head from side to side, letting her hair float like thick black molasses around her face. She spent a few more minutes diving and surfacing before soaping down and scrubbing her supple body until it hurt only from the rough cleansing being dealt it, and not from long hours in the saddle.

She passed the soap sensuously over small firm breasts and down a flat belly and muscular thighs, and longed to be held and loved. It had been forever since she had been in anyone's arms. She did not count the sheriffs or deputies or bankers. She did not even think of them. That had been business — not love. They had been Anglos — not Mexicans.

She set the soap down on a rock and swam slowly around the pool until all the suds had been washed from her hair and body. Floating on her back, she looked up at the stars and the moon suspended in the black night and thought back to four days ago. She remembered the brave blue-eyed lady angrily saying: "Do you want to kiss me too?" Margarita chuckled at the stars. What a joke to have played on the Americano. To have jumped quickly from her horse, grabbed the lady and, like a wild bandito with much *macho*, kissed her full red lips. Then to have ripped from her own face her bandanna to reveal to the Anglo how she had been tricked by her own words. Strangely, to think of her lips on the beautiful lady's almost made Margarita warm between her legs. It *had* been a long time since she had been loved.

She closed her eyes against the moonlight and imagined what it would be like to kiss the lady. Such an unusual idea, one she would never have thought of but for the question from the woman herself. It annoyed her and her mind drifted to other things.

Soon afterward, Margarita left the pool and returned to her cabin. She lit a lantern and sat at the table for a while, staring into its light. Although still hungry, she was rested and refreshed, and freshly clothed in a lighter, checkered blouse of cotton and pants of denim. She was content.

Her thoughts drifted to the events of two years ago, and her decision to become a bandito. She had made the decision in no time at all as her house and barns full of cotton and horses burned to the ground while she stood watching Seth swinging from the tree and listened to the horses shriek in mortal terror and pain, stinking the air with their burning flesh. To be a Mexican married to an Americano was deeply resented by some. The cold-blooded act of killing her husband had proved it forevermore.

She had immediately formulated a plan, carrying it forward that very day. She had first buried Seth, then dug up the money from beneath the stone hearth in the kitchen where they had always cached their ever growing profits, not trusting the banks. Lastly she had donned men's clothes, bought a horse, and headed for Loma Parda.

She shook her head to clear it of these past memories, memories that made her burn with a vengeful fire. She did not want to feel furor now. She wanted to feel peace. She allowed previous restful sensation to return.

She sat on the edge of the cot, taking off only her boots and outer pants, tossing them carelessly aside before dousing the lantern. Later she would deal with her plunder which still lay untouched on the table.

She lay down without covers, letting sleep slowly overtake her, its healing gift gently loosening tense muscles around the perpetual downward pull of her mouth. Her eyes closed and she began to breathe quietly. Finally asleep, strong muscles became softly feminine now that the day had let go its tight hold on her. She rolled over on her side once and did not move again until morning.

Chapter Three

It had been three weeks since the stagecoach holdup. Margarita had been gratefully alone for almost the entire time. Two days after they returned to the meadow, the men had left, as they usually did after a job, moving out late at night.

Margarita knew they had gone to Sourdough, an area the law normally stayed clear of, a mean and safe little town some forty miles east of the meadow. There they would squander or gamble away every last dollar they had stolen and give away the jewelry in exchange for favors from the ladies. The three would spend their time at a dirty little hole-in-the-wall saloon that didn't ask where payment for its bad whiskey and tired women came from.

Margarita didn't mind being left alone for long periods of time. She preferred the solitude, and it gave her an opportunity to carefully hide her plunder. One day not long after the discovery of the meadow, and at a time when the men were away, she had decided to investigate the area above the pool. To her delight, she had spied a small cave, one that might have been inhabited during some ancient time. She scooted back to her cabin, returning quickly with a lantern. She had explored further, learning that the shelter had indeed been used by a people in some distant past. She had found scattered pieces of broken pottery, a circular carving that made no sense to her chiseled into the side of a wall, soot on the ceiling from long dead fires, and small bones, probably left by mountain lions or bear. She estimated that a family, perhaps two families, had shared this refuge. Disturbing nothing, she had wrapped her cache in an oil cloth and then stashed it behind a large rock deep in the back of the cavern. Since then, she was careful to first check the cave before entering, knowing it was an ideal place for animals to hide and rest.

She rose leisurely this morning to a brilliant early morning sun. Clouds billowed in thick white piles reaching thousands of feet into the atmosphere, unidentifiable giants bumping into the distant purple mountains of the Sangre de Cristo range stretching to the south. Turkey vultures soared majestically in large, sweeping circles. Margarita stood motionless in the doorway, inhaling the scent of wild mint and sweet clover. Hummingbirds fed at the veins of scarlet beardtongue running through the high grasses of the meadow.

Butterflies flitted everywhere, lighting briefly on a single blade or blossom only to take flight again. The horses at the far end of the spacious field grazed contentedly in the still, clear air.

She climbed the path to the pool to take a quick dip in icy cold water not yet warmed by the day's sun. Finished, she vigorously rubbed down with a rough towel before climbing back into her warm clothes and then headed up to the cave to hide her stolen possessions.

As a group, she and the men had done well in the time that they had ridden together. No one had been shot, and they had made at least fair hauls almost every time.

She had not selected where to rebuild her life. Perhaps down in Lincoln County, where she and Seth had once lived. She wanted to raise horses and possibly try her hand at raising corn and beans. But this time there would be a certain difference on her farm. This time there would be heavily armed guards — with orders to shoot to kill should anyone ever again come near her or her land.

As she exited the cave, a sensation of well-being filled her. Suddenly and sharply her amiable mood was interrupted by a loud shout from below. With a dark surge of despair she realized that the men had returned from Sourdough. With a comforting caress across her scar, she glanced a final time at the dark and peaceful cave.

As she headed down the path, her steps lagged and her heart felt heavy, the morning's brilliance seemingly gone in a flash. That time had come again — the time to start thinking about their next job. She did not look forward to it. She bolstered herself by thinking of the coming robbery as yet another step toward an end to outlawing and running with these men.

She reached the bottom of the trail just as they finished turning their mounts out to pasture.

"Margarita," Bill called out. "How're the hosses?"

Inwardly Margarita cursed the man. She could be lying injured in his path and still Bill's first concern would be the welfare of the animals. It has always been hers, as well. He asked the question every time he returned from Sourdough, doubting her ability to take care of the horses. She was as capable as he, any day. "Everything is fine," she answered crossly.

"We'll meet in an hour," Bert announced abruptly, and turned to follow the others walking silently toward the men's cabin.

Margarita went to her own cabin, her mind totally focused on the coming discussion. She made breakfast over a small fire just outside the door. Straddling a large flat log which served both as table and chair, she prepared a tortilla, the flour made only yesterday from parboiled corn kernels soaked in lime water and then ground between a heavy stone roller and a slab of rock. Absently she added fresh water, then patted the mixture between her palms until it was thin and round. After frying it, she filled the tortilla with thick, crisp bacon and beans, and ate from a metal plate resting on the rough bark in front of her. She licked her fingers clean when she had finished and sat staring into space, idly chewing on a dried peach, rinsing down the last morsel of food with coffee, the grains having sufficiently boiled and settled to the bottom of the pot.

Deep in thought about the group's present method of operation, she concluded that they would be wise to change their habits, something she had been reflecting over for a couple of weeks now. Too many stagecoaches had been hit by them lately; seven since last fall. Their good fortune could not continue forever. She would suggest a bank holdup or a train robbery — far from here.

This area was getting too dangerous. If they continued to push, even their secure hideaway would no longer be secure. Eventually it would be discovered — by luck, just as they themselves had found it, if for no other reason.

She walked over to the cistern positioned against the foot of the westside cliff and rinsed her plate clean beneath its overflow. Leaning over its edge, she sucked water into her mouth, feeling the icy cold liquid slide down her throat, slice through her chest, then enter her belly. She had just taken another big mouthful when she heard Sam call to her from the doorway of the men's cabin.

Wiping her dripping mouth on a cotton sleeve, she waved indicating that she had heard him. Leaving the plate on the log by her cabin, she joined the others already gathered at the table.

She could never adjust to the heavy unpleasant aroma these men emitted. In the small room it seemed to permeate the air and everything within. As much as she had loved Seth, she had never gotten used to his smell, the oppressive male muskiness of him. At times, it had seemed to very nearly clog her nostrils, especially during their most intimate moments.

She flopped on the edge of a cot as Bert asked, "Well, who has an idea, here?"

"There's a stage comin' through Windwhistle Pass next week that ain't a regular," Sam commented. "Found that out from a girlie for a brooch." Grinning as if he had performed some noble deed on the group's behalf, he noisily sucked on a small stick.

Margarita looked at the floor so that he would not see the loathing in her eyes for the way he used women and openly bragged about it. It made no difference that Sam was her protector from time to time.

Bert struck a match on the heel of his boot, the movement causing his silver spur to jingle, a pleasant sound strangely out of place in these crude surroundings. Smoke from a rolled cigarette clamped tightly between his teeth rose in a thin, blue line as he lighted it. "Got any other ideas?" he asked.

Margarita sat up from her slumped position. "No more stages. There have been too many this past year."

The men looked her way but did not interrupt. During planning, each member had an equal voice and so the rest listened to the woman speaking now.

She continued, "We must change our territory or our method. How many wanted posters did you see on your way to Sourdough?"

"Quite a few on the way," Bill replied. "Nary a one on the way back." He laughed at his own joke.

Frowning, Margarita said scornfully, "Ripping them down does nothing. Everyone still looks for a four-member gang in this area. We should move to new territory. This means giving up the meadow. Otherwise a bank or a train would be all we should go after. For a while at least. And far from here — on fast horses."

"You know, boys," Bert agreed, nodding thoughtfully, "she's right. But I'm not for givin' up the meadow. Okay, no more stages. That's exactly what the law's lookin' for — stagecoach robbers."

"Go for the train, then," Sam proposed.

"Too much work," Bill grunted.

"Then it's the bank," Margarita told them.

"Hell, no," Bill argued. "Too many people to see you by daylight. Too many cowhands at night. There must be somethin' easier we could do."

Perturbed that he would not readily accept the bank as their next target she said, "I never thought you were a coward, Bill."

He was on top of her in an instant. "You little bitch," he snarled only inches from her face. Rough, hairy hands clutched at her throat to squeeze the life out of her. A knee pressed painfully into her chest, driving her into the cot.

Suddenly the pain lessened; the wild-eyed outlaw's hands were ripped violently from her throat. Sam had yanked him off her chest and unceremoniously thrown him to the floor.

"That bitch better keep her yap shut," Bill raged through gritted teeth, "or I'll kill her." His eyes bulged with hatred as he rose unsteadily to his feet and moved to a stool. Margarita struggled to breathe.

Bert reached out and dealt Bill a stinging slap across the mouth. "Shut up, damn you! We're here to work, not fight. I'll beat the shit outta the two of you," he warned, glaring at them both. "We'll do as Margarita said: hit a bank. Margarita, you go on up to Colter. The railroad runs through there, it's a cattle pickup. That'll mean big money in the vault. See if it makes sense to take the bank, and how we can do it. Find out what's goin' on."

Still gasping for breath, unable to speak, Margarita pulled herself up into a sitting position and nodded, rubbing her bruised throat. She would be glad to go to Colter. It would be a relief to be parted from these animals so soon again.

She walked — almost staggered — back to her cabin.

She sat on the edge of her bed. One day she would deal with Bill. He would be made to pay the same way those she helped rob had paid. He would feel every unkindness he had ever put her through.

By contrast, Bert's easy agreement about robbing a bank had surprised Margarita. Colter was a five-day journey northeast of here. Apparently he had been thinking the same thing as she: it was time to put distance between the hideout and their next job. At times Margarita almost admired Bert's judgment.

She went outside to sit on the log, letting the warmth of the noon sun beat against her back while she thought through what she must do to prepare for tonight's journey; the clothing she would need, the right amount of food, plenty of extra ammunition in case she ran into trouble, and lastly, the horse she could most afford to give up. There would be no suggestions made by the others, no last minute advice. Certainly no wishes of good luck would be offered.

She packed a pair of saddlebags in the afternoon, then lay down until evening, speaking to no one. Just before the moon rose, she buckled on her gun belt and mounted up. Her horse and the lonesome creaking of saddle leather were her only companions as she left the meadow behind and entered the canyon which would take her to the valley below.

It was completely black within the canyon's walls, and she wisely let her mount pick his own way down the trail. She listened to water fall to the floor of the chasm, its near vertical sides selfishly squeezing out the heavily mineralized fluid drop by single drop, and the lonesome clip-clop of the horse's shoes echoing against the walls with each step. Always cold and damp, and doubly so at night, the wind blowing up from the bottom of the winding path forced her to draw her hat low over her face and pull her thick coat tighter around her.

The uncomfortable pressure of the collar against her still tender throat brought memory again of Bill's hands wrapped around her neck. Why, she wondered as she rubbed her scar, were men so rough? Why did they lie and cheat and steal and kill? Women didn't do those things. Not many women, that is. And she hadn't killed anyone yet. But she acted out of revenge. What revenge did the rest of the gang seek? None that she knew of. They were motivated only by greed.

Her mind sought images of a kind man, one like her father who had treated her well. She could think only of Seth. His kindness was why she had married him. But even he had not taken time to find out how she thought or what she thought about.

Women should live together, she decided as her horse continued to seek his way cautiously down the trail. Men should be there only when needed: to father children, to ride the range, to do the heavy work. Otherwise, they should stay away.

But, Margarita told herself, the women couldn't keep each other warm at night. A woman couldn't fill another with love until her mind was gone and her soul was stolen. Unexpectedly, the image of flinging herself off her horse and into the arms of the Americano woman popped into her mind.

A pleasurable tremor passed through her, and she hung her head and closed her eyes against the canyon's inky blackness, concentrating fiercely on the sounds around her; the dripping water, the angle at which the horse traveled, the feel of her collar against her throat, the slight pain that it caused.

But then her mind insisted: a woman would never hurt another woman, as Bill — and other men at times — had hurt her; not deliberately — not knowingly.

"Damn it!" she muttered fiercely, and began to hum a tuneless song so that she would not think anymore.

In half an hour she left the narrower canyon for the larger one, the fast pace of its water sounding ten times as loud at night as it did in the light of day. Prudently, she pulled her horse to a halt. It wouldn't pay just to dash out through the shrubs and onto the trail. Even now, someone could be hiding nearby. But in a few moments she decided she was safe and began the four-day journey she would take on horseback before switching to stagecoach.

An experienced lone horsewoman from countless past surveys, she was unafraid. She had learned to read signs well and knew instinctively when danger was near. She traveled only by night and slept by day, hiding just before the break of dawn among trees or within a small gulch or dry arroyo. She drank from cold streams and ate pemmican and beef jerky, confining herself to a dry camp, not chancing discovery through smoke from a fire. And when she started out again the next evening, she never left a mark that she had been there.

She traveled north for two nights before crossing Tequesquite Creek. The third night, she crossed Ute Creek, then cut directly northeast. Early into her fourth night on the trail, she saw the distant lights of Dusty Springs, the first town she must enter to carry out her plan.

In the gloom of night, she barely made out a pile of rocks in an open area, silhouetted some distance to her right. Riding over to it, she wished the moon were more helpful, but clouds had moved in to block its light almost completely.

She dismounted to study the rock pile from all sides. Yes, it would do. She found a stout stick long enough to poke among the rocks, searching for a hiding place free of rattlers and large enough to jam in the saddle, bags, and blankets. When she found a good spot, she breathed a sigh of relief, whispering a quiet prayer of thanks that she hadn't disturbed any night creatures. One bite by a rattler or a scorpion and she would be finished right where she stood.

She stripped the horse of everything. She hugged his neck and leaned against his warm body. "Go home, Dusty," she said, not knowing if he would or not. She slapped his rump and listened to his hoofbeats recede into the night. Turning to her tasks, she forced her bridle and saddle in between the wide crack she had chosen earlier. From the saddlebags she pulled out a dress, stockings, underwear, shoes, handbag, a small hat. She stripped quickly, shoving her men's clothing into the bags, then donned the women's attire, shivering in the dark.

Jamming the saddlebags in with the rest of the gear, she rolled a rock over the opening, grunting and straining with the effort. She found a few dead pieces of shrubbery and threw them on top of the rock. Using tumbleweed, she brushed away her tracks. From the light of the moon revealed through parted clouds, the place looked as natural as she could make it. It would have to do.

She shook the wrinkles and dust from the skirt of her dark blue dress and smoothed its snug fitting top against her body. She combed her hair, tying it in a bun at the base of her neck. Throwing a woolen shawl across her shoulders, then pinning on the hat, she felt she was ready. The small handbag over her arm, she began the walk toward town a good mile away brushing out her tracks with a tumbleweed she dragged behind her.

She kept a careful watch all around. It wouldn't do for a lady to be seen strolling alone outside the town's limits at this hour.

Arriving at the outskirts of Dusty Springs forty-five minutes later, Margarita entered the town and casually stepped onto a wooden sidewalk as if she had merely been taking in a breath of fresh air at the far end of the street. The worst that might happen was that the sheriff would think her a lady of the night, which was likely with her crumpled clothing. When she got to a hotel she would let the dress hang overnight to help rid it of some of its wrinkles.

She began to search for the nearest café. There she could probably learn when the stagecoach would leave for Colter. Once aboard, there would be no problem traveling. She would be just another passenger.

She passed closed shops and open saloons. Mounted men in wide brimmed hats and rough garb, wearing low slung pistols, rode in groups, dismounting to enter the already jam-packed public houses. Others stood in clusters speaking Spanish or English, talking and spitting and rolling cigarettes, their loud laughter filling the air. She heard a shot or two, a tinny piano as she walked by a saloon's batwing doors. Somewhere off on a side street someone strummed a mournful guitar.

Entering a small café empty of customers, she sat at a table near the door. The red and white checkered tablecloth had countless stains on it, and the windows' matching curtains were heavy with dust. A tired looking waitress came from behind the counter to take her order.

When her late night supper arrived, Margarita asked about the stage.

"Seven in the morning," the waitress replied uninterestedly. "Front of the bank."

Margarita thanked her and began to eat a thick steak and boiled potatoes, relishing her meal, paying no heed to the dirt on the rim of the coffee cup. She had dined under far worse conditions than these, and it had been days since she had had a decent meal.

She took a room at the town's only hotel, ignoring the clerk's sneer. She knew what he was thinking. A woman with no luggage wasn't taking a room to sleep.

She lit a bedside lantern and walked over to the room's single window to pull down a torn shade. She removed only her hat, shoes, and dress, giving the garment a good shake before hanging it on the back of the yellowed, paint-chipped door. She squatted uncomfortably over the chamber pot, not daring to sit on it, certain the thing hadn't seen a rinsing in a month.

She chose to sleep in her underwear and stockings rather than let the dingy gray sheets touch her skin. Finally settled, she turned out the lantern. Sleep softened the hard lines around her eyes and mouth, and she dreamed of nothing.

Chapter Four

The land between Dusty Springs and Colter began to change to a gentler, more rolling terrain. Although there were still stacks of rocks scattered across the land and tall mountains in the distance, there were also many more trees. Fewer gulches had to be crossed by bridge, indicating less soil erosion here than south of Dusty Springs and all the way back to the meadow.

But it was still a hot, dusty ride for Margarita and the two male passengers. The four-mule team pulled the stagecoach rapidly over the rough road, bouncing and jostling them throughout the long, uncomfortable day. Rolling down the canvas curtains had not deterred the grit which seeped into the coach, seeking out the tired travelers. Dirt flowed in through the windows, flying everywhere. The leather seat made Margarita's back and bottom sweat unbearably, and she longed to be rid of the binding pettiskirt and dress and high-buttoned, tight-fitting shoes.

During their only stop Margarita skipped eating lunch at the crude swing station to find a tree to hide behind before vomiting, so motion-sick had she become. Her traveling companions offered their sympathies but she ignored them, suspicious of their kindness.

With the stage rolling once more, she lapsed into a tired doze as the swaying and shaking vehicle finished its final twenty miles.

Arriving in Colter at dusk, Margarita went immediately to the nearest hotel. With only sleep on her mind she was unable to admire the surprisingly large sprawling town with its wide main street and one and two-story buildings.

Unlike last night's hotel, this one was clean, offering a pleasant second-story room with two windows facing the main street. The room contained a comfortable bed with clean linen, a simple stand and dresser, and a single chair. On the dresser was a bowl and a pitcher filled with fresh water. Three lamps sat about, and Margarita lit them all. Wearily she scrubbed away the day's dust, doused the lanterns, then lay down nude without covers in spite of the chill in the air.

Bert had once mentioned that he had been to Colter, but Margarita had not imagined that the place was this big — a bigness due, no doubt, to the railroad's shipping cattle north, from all around New Mexico Territory.

Already situated on the Beaver River, this town with a railroad was certain to survive and grow. That meant big money flowing into the area. If the bank were to be robbed, the gang would probably do very well.

Further thoughts of her own potential wealth were cut off mid-stream as blessed sleep soon claimed her tired mind.

Margarita woke to a loud knock on the door. "Your bath, ma'am," a male voice called.

It took her a moment to recall where she was, that last night she had ordered a bath for this morning. She jumped up and wrapped a blanket tightly around herself and padded to the door to let in a young man who dragged with him a large galvanized tub. "I'll be right back with the water, ma'am," he told her, politely avoiding looking at her. A few minutes later he returned with two other big boys, each carrying large oak buckets of hot water.

After they had emptied their burdens, Margarita thanked them, then closed and locked the door. She dropped the blanket to the floor and stepped into the tub to sink contentedly into the steaming water, to soak away the days of travel and dirt from her body. She sat with propped knees, her eyes closed, her head resting on the tub's edge until the water began to lose its heat. Then she quickly scrubbed down, rinsed, and only reluctantly climbed out.

She stopped briefly at the desk to have the tub removed, then walked out into a sunlit day. Hitching rails in front of whitewashed saloons with large, gaudily painted signs hawking their attractions were already lined with horses. Men's and women's apparel shops and stores with high false fronts were open, selling hardware, guns, footwear, and housewares. Mounted riders rode by, along with buggies and wagons drawn by single horses or teams. Mexicans, Anglos, and Indians crowded the sidewalks. Businessmen stood talking in small groups. Ladies in colorful dresses with parasols draped casually over their shoulders strolled by. Hurrying cowboys intent either on business or pleasure passed her, politely tiping their hats. Delicious odors of cooking food drifted her way as she walked by several eating establishments, some simple, others a bit more grand. The ringing of the smithy's hammer sounded to her left as she wandered to the furthest end of town where four branching streets held a few more small shops with the proprietors' homes built directly above. There were well kept wood sidewalks the entire length of the main street, and stone walks in front of some of the side shops.

As busy as Colter was this morning, last night it had looked even more so. It appeared to Margarita far more possible to take the bank by day rather than by night.

She put business aside for a moment and took time to eat a full breakfast at one of the smaller restaurants. She needed to be well fed and rested if she were to think this job through properly.

She went to a women's clothing shop and selected a large carpetbag, three dresses, two blouses with matching skirts, two hats, undergarments, and a cream-colored parasol that struck her fancy. She ordered her purchases to be delivered to the hotel immediately. She stopped at the shoe shop and bought two pairs of soft leather shoes, very comfortable and very expensive. She paid for everything happily, with stolen cash.

She loved shopping for women's clothing and would make sure she wore each new garment at least once. When it was time to return to the meadow, she would cram the wardrobe, with the exception of a pair of shoes and the dress she would be wearing, into the carpetbag, eventually hiding the bag where she had stashed her saddle and bags. She would be on horseback again and did not dare add extra bulk and weight to an unproven horse should she need to ride him hard.

Hurrying back to the hotel, her new shoes tucked under an arm, she found the delivery boy waiting in the lobby. The packages deposited in her room, she cast aside her well worn attire with an excited squeal. She selected from her new wardrobe the lemon-colored dress trimmed with white lace at cuffs and collar. Her dark skin glowed against the bright yellow of the dress. Humming a tune, she pulled on her fine shoes. She decided against wearing a hat, preferring to carry only the parasol.

Looking into the mirror, she tucked away a strand of stray hair that had worked itself loose from her carefully combed bun. She was not yet satisfied. No wardrobe was truly complete without perfume. For that she would go to the drugstore.

She entered the quiet building, empty of clerk or customer, the store's only sound the musical tinkle of the warning bell as she opened the door. Shelves aligning the walls of the long and narrow room were heavily stocked with rows and rows of patented medicines in dark brown vessels, white porcelain containers, and gold-colored tins decorated with swirling scrolls and fine lettering. Candy in large jars sat on countertops alongside books, children's trinkets and women's whatnots. There, too, were the perfumes displayed in fancy bottles on a notions counter.

Without waiting for assistance, Margarita helped herself to the vessels, smelling of each with eyes closed. Intent upon her fourth sample and enjoying its rose-scented fragrance, she was slightly startled when a voice at her side said, "May I help you?"

Margarita turned toward her assistant. "Yes, thank you, I was interested in —" Her words cut off in her throat as her gaze fell upon the brave Americano lady she had robbed weeks ago.

She knew she must conceal her surprise, but she could feel her heart thumping and her hands beginning to shake as the woman continued to look at her.

"I was interested in this perfume," Margarita finished, wanting only to get out of there.

"Let me show you another," the woman offered, placing her hand in a friendly fashion on Margarita's arm.

The light pressure of her touch seemed to burn through the fabric of Margarita's blouse, holding her there. Before she could refuse, another small bottle of golden liquid was held out for her inspection.

Margarita glanced down at the smooth skin of the Anglo's slender hand, the well groomed nails. The hand was as flawless as Margarita's own was rough. She reached for the bottle, careful to avoid touching the delicate fingers that held the tiny vessel.

The woman walked behind the counter to pull several more from a shelf beneath, displaying them before her anxious customer. "This," she said, choosing a tall slender bottle, "is our loveliest."

Margarita mumbled thanks and opened it. Pretending great interest, she quickly swabbed a dab on her wrist, then smelled the perfume. "It's lovely," she agreed. "I'll take it." It was almost impossible not to bolt out the door as she waited for the package to be wrapped.

Margarita watched and felt the caress of slim fingers against her palm as her change was counted into her hand. The contact left her confused. She hated herself for

39

feeling pleasure — not fury — at the touch of the Americano. She glanced up and found the woman staring intently at her, a slight frown creasing her forehead. There dwelt within the deep blue eyes a question. Margarita did not dare guess what it might be.

The tense moment was interrupted by the opening of the door. The bell's tinkle was nearly drowned out by a loud, deep voice: "Julia, where's Henry?" A large bearded man held a smaller companion by the shoulders, half dragging him through the doorway. "Where is he?" he asked again. His burden bled heavily from the right arm.

"Not here today," Julia answered, turning her attention to the badly injured cowboy. "Bring him over here." She ran from behind the counter and grabbed a chair from the rear of the room. "He's seriously hurt. Where's Doctor James?"

"Out," came the gruff answer. Together the two eased the young man into the chair. Margarita saw the bearded man's badge pinned to his shirt. "Can you fix him up?" he asked, not even glancing Margarita's way.

"I'll see what I can do," Julia replied. "But he doesn't look good."

"Just do your best," the lawman said.

Unflinchingly, she began to tear away the sleeve from the cowboy's bloody wound, speaking soothing words as he moaned in pain. Margarita left the store.

Often Margarita used whomever she needed to gain information that she couldn't learn on her own, so running into the sheriff had hardly disturbed her now. However, running into the brave lady had been very nearly terrifying, she had scrutinized Margarita so.

But still — how exciting to see her again.

And how insane, you fool, she chided herself. The woman is an Americano! Unconsciously, she smoothed her scarred eyebrow.

She entered a small restaurant to order coffee. As she sipped the strong black liquid heavily sweetened with sugar, she dwelt upon the chance meeting between herself and the saleswoman, wondering how she had come to be on the stage that day, so far from Colter. Had one of the other passengers been her husband? No, no one had come to her aid to protectively hush the sharp-tongued lady. Why, then, would she travel alone?

Finished with her coffee, and with many questions still unanswered, she left the restaurant to stroll the busy streets. She had other things — more important things — to think of than this Anglo, and she began by noting with business-like efficiency how many people roamed about.

She would stay in Colter at least a week, perhaps longer. She could tell by then which day had the least number of people in town. Today did not appear to be that day.

An hour later she was satisfied that she had noted all the buildings and alleys, all the possible entrances and exits into and out of Colter. She would take additional walks to familiarize herself more fully with the town, but for now she had seen enough.

In a couple of days she would go to the bank. Under pretense of opening a small savings account, she would study the interior of the tall one-story brick building and observe its activities.

She rented a buggy in the afternoon and took a long drive, searching for hiding places should the gang need one. She discovered three possibilities; the first, a small amphitheater hidden between two large sloping hills and banked against a steep rock wall. If found there, the gang would be trapped, but the place would do in a pinch; they could scale the left side of the hill and hide among the pines that grew thick and tall all the way to the top, several hundred feet above. The second location was a deep slash in the earth that four riders could easily hide within if they escaped fast enough, with plenty of flat rock around the gully to hide their immediate tracks. The third spot was an old shack about two miles south of town. It would be a place to make a last stand, but that was all.

She would take future rides, looking for still more avenues of safety. Robbing banks was a thousand times more chancy than robbing a stagecoach — but much more profitable.

With the afternoon nearly gone, she returned to town and bought a newspaper in the lobby of the hotel. After a late lunch, she went to her room for the remainder of the evening.

She entertained herself with the paper, struggling with its English words. Occasionally she stood gazing out of the window. With a surge of pleasure she saw Julia pass by on the other side of the street. How regal she looked; how in control.

Margarita had wanted to return to the drugstore to talk to her when she got back from her drive. She had even considered the idea, but involvement with anyone was too dangerous. People remembered little things about you even after five minutes' time. She couldn't afford that. It was dangerous enough becoming involved with sheriffs and bankers without adding more complication. But at another time, in another place. . . .

When it became dark, Margarita did not light the lanterns, but instead stood at the window in the darkened room, gazing at the people passing below. She watched until nearly two in the morning. For the next four nights she did the same. Two no-nonsense looking deputies patrolled hourly, and except for patrons of the saloons, there was no other traffic.

Every man wore a weapon on his hip at night — not the case during the day. In daytime most cowboys had guns but most businessmen did not, she observed; nor shop or store owners. Women did not count. Yes, daylight cut down drastically on readily available firearms.

The weapons were there, she knew. But it would take time to grab one from a drawer or beneath a counter, run out of a store, aim, and shoot. Those few extra seconds would slow down the citizens of Colter enough that the gang, on their fastest horses, could very possibly be out of range. Daylight still looked best to strike. Now to select the slowest day.

She found two excuses to enter the bank, taking careful scrutiny both times of the interior as well as the vault, a large walk-in room with a heavy metal door. Seeing its intricate structure clinched it for Margarita. At night there would be no way they could blow apart all that metal, empty the chamber, and clear out before the entire town was upon them.

The bank's interior, high-ceilinged and airy, had plenty of room for people to conduct their business, and even a few chairs against the walls for the convenience of those who wished to rest while waiting their turn. High on the rear wall was a large mural of a man and his wife and children enjoying a picnic on a cloudless day, the family sitting beneath a tall tree in a spacious field filled with colorful flowers, the man and his wife staring down upon the depositors with friendly eyes while the children sat a few feet away petting a little dog. The work was well

43

done and very lifelike and gave the bank's interior a look of warmth and welcome.

There was no guard inside, but she knew that the three tellers who worked behind barred windows had pistols within easy reach, probably on a shelf just beneath the cash drawers. Sam and Bill and Bert could take care of that problem easily enough.

By the ninth day she had gathered all the information she needed. The stage left that morning for Dusty Springs, and in an hour and a half she would be on it.

For the journey, she wore her favorite dress, the yellow full-skirted one that fit snugly around her upper body but billowed comfortably at the sleeves and waist. She refused to feel the loss of having to give up her other beautiful things as she tightly jammed each piece of clothing into the carpetbag. She was becoming exceptionally good at burying painful moments in her life.

Before leaving, Margarita went to one of the better dining establishments in town where she had eaten once before. She ordered a large breakfast, eating every last scrap of eggs, fried potatoes, and a thick slab of beef. She was uncomfortable from stuffing herself, but she wouldn't eat this well again in a long time, not even if she cooked it herself. And, she vowed, she would not throw up from today's travels.

She had just drained her final cup of coffee when Julia entered the restaurant. Margarita felt her throat tighten as Julia glanced her way, a warm smile flooding her face. Without hesitation, she walked over to Margarita's table. Margarita was glad enough to see her, but this woman's friendliness frightened her and she wasn't sure why. Nor did she like it. She did not feel in control.

"Good morning," Julia said, still smiling brilliantly. She was dressed for the day's work in a starched white blouse tucked into a simple black skirt. She managed to make the plain clothing look rich and full. She wore her hair gathered in the back, the golden tresses falling slightly over her forehead and gently covering her ears. Margarita pulled her gaze away.

"Good morning." Margarita rose. "I have to catch the stage."

"I was going to ask if I could join you." Julia checked a tiny gold watch that hung from a slim chain around her neck. "The stage doesn't leave for half an hour, and it's only a short walk from here."

Margarita looked again at this woman who sounded so damnably sincere. She found herself liking Julia and hating herself for it.

"Just long enough for coffee?"

Margarita knew she should not spend another minute longer here. Not a single, solitary minute.

Her slight pause was enough for Julia to say, "Good, I was hoping you would," and she put an assuming hand on Margarita's arm.

As they both sat, Julia offered an apology. "I'm sorry I had to leave you so abruptly the other day. Sheriff Hoskins is forever dragging in some poor soul whenever Doc James is out of town, or Henry, who owns the store, doesn't happen to come in that day."

"Is the man all right?" Margarita asked. She didn't give a damn if the man was all right or not. She just wanted to leave. Then why the hell did you sit back down, she silently questioned herself.

"He'll recover," Julia declared with a slight, lilting laugh, holding Margarita firmly to the chair. "But he won't be as big a man in the Lucky Dice Saloon as he once thought he was. You're new here, aren't you?" she asked.

"I know just about everyone in town and the surrounding ranches."

"I'm Margarita Sanchez. I'm just visiting friends."

"And my name is Julia Blake. A cup of coffee before you go? My treat." A few minutes later the waitress delivered Margarita her third cup, and eggs and buttered toast to Julia.

Margarita was now convinced she had made a grave error remaining seated with this woman. There was no room in her heart for anything but scorn and dislike for Anglos. And yet, she did feel something else. She couldn't help it. When Julia spoke, it was as if Margarita was listening again to the beautiful music from a fine cherry wood music box she had once heard as a child. As Julia smiled, her face took on more brightness than the midsummer day's sun. She sighed softly, and the sound was more gentle than the wind that caressed the boughs of the trees that clung to the mountainsides of the meadow.

Abruptly, rudely, Margarita stood. "I must go."

"But there's still time," Julia protested. "Stay a little longer."

"No," Margarita said more sharply than she meant to. "I don't want to miss the stage."

"Yes, of course."

Margarita heard a twinge of sadness in Julia's voice. It couldn't be helped. Another minute with this woman and Margarita would never forget her — nor want to. *Dios,* an Anglo as a friend? Unthinkable!

She hastened away from the restaurant.

The stage arrived in Dusty Springs that evening with Margarita battling wave after wave of nausea. She stayed in the same wretched hotel as before, wanting to slap the stinking leer from the clerk's familiar face. She had luggage with her this time. There was no reason for him to look at her like that. She shot him dead with her eyes and felt better as he turned away from her non-yielding and penetrating gaze.

Early the next morning she again donned the yellow dress. She rented a buggy, telling the stablehand that she wouldn't be back for a couple of days; she had been invited to visit the Rocking-B Spread.

She had learned of the Rocking-B's existence the day before while listening to two of her traveling companions chat during the long and unpleasant return trip to Dusty Springs. One of the gentlemen even politely pointed it out as the stage rolled by. It was only five miles east of town — not an unreasonable distance for a lone woman to travel in a buggy. Unwittingly, the two men had helped her come up with an excuse to conveniently obtain a horse without having to put any effort into inventing a scheme of her own.

Margarita put that useful information to work now. No one would look for her for at least the next two days. When they finally became concerned and rode to the ranch to see why the rig had not yet been returned, she would be miles and days away, heading in the opposite direction.

She drove toward the Rocking-B for half an hour before turning off the road, and wound between and around hills and trees in the area looking for a place to stop for the day. Just to be doubly sure she wouldn't be seen, she drove for another half mile before she made her selection. The buggy teetered dangerously as Margarita guided it slowly over the edge of a deep gully. Once on the bottom, she breathed a sigh of relief and jumped down quickly, going to the horse and patting him affectionately for a job well done.

The location of the rock pile where she had stashed her saddle and bags was too far away and the land too flat to return to now. Taking advantage of the time left until dark, she sat in the lee of the gulch resting in what little shade there was.

She mulled over what she had learned over the past two weeks. Aside from her success in finding the setup for the robbery, she had been pleased when Julia had sat with her at breakfast, disturbing though it had been. She couldn't remember feeling that good about seeing anyone since Seth had courted her. Neither could she remember experiencing that height of excitement at any time he had come to see her.

Suddenly angered with herself for her unusual feelings, for having revived such pleasant sensations from times long dead, she leaned back against a rock to doze until nightfall.

As soon as it was dark, Margarita left the buggy behind and, after collecting the carpetbag, mounted the horse bareback, hitched her dress to her waist, nudged the gelding into motion, and guided him onto the plains under the light of a pale moon.

At a steady trot, she returned to the rock pile, widely skirting Dusty Springs. She grunted with the effort of retrieving her gear. A quick check showed everything still in order except for her food. Something had crawled into the saddlebags and helped itself to at least half of it. The rest was only slightly nibbled on. She just wouldn't think about it whenever she ate.

She changed into men's attire, stuffed the clothing she had been wearing into the bags, then strapped on her revolver, securing the holster to her thigh with leather thongs. Exchanging the stable's bridle for her own, she saddled the horse quickly and expertly. After tying down the blanket roll and bags, she poked the extra bridle into the opening along with the carpetbag. Pausing only a moment to look into the black crack where the carpetbag holding her lovely clothing could not longer be seen, she sighed once, then shoved the rock fully into place. She brushed out her tracks, then mounted up in a single graceful movement.

It felt good to be in the saddle again. Drawing her hat low over her eyes, she kicked the horse into a trot, listening to the creak of saddle leather and enjoying the feel of the gelding's rhythmic motion beneath her.

Four nights later, she was safely back at the meadow.

Chapter Five

On the afternoon following her return from Colter, the men and Margarita gathered together in front of her cabin. In the warm sunshine Bill and Sam lounged against the building while Margarita and Bert straddled the log. Margarita had just spent the last half hour explaining in detail all she had learned about Colter.

"It sounds too easy," Bill growled.

"An' too risky if you ask me," Sam added. "Five days to get there, five back. All those folks runnin' around town durin' the holdup."

"I'm telling you it can be done," Margarita pronounced. "There is no guard, but no doubt the tellers have guns handy. Thursday, the town had the fewest people in the bank and on the streets. We'll take along extra horses; our fastest ones. It won't take five days getting home on those animals. Besides, we could stand the law off forever from the meadow if we had to. You know that."

"If we make it back," Bill spat.

"I don't know, Margarita," Bert responded slowly. "I never heard of a bank in a town of that size without some sort'a guard." He took off his stained hat and ran a knarled hand through matted hair. "There's gotta be somebody there someplace."

"There was no one," she answered emphatically, "except the tellers."

If the gang could take this bank, there was a good chance she would have all the money she needed to buy new land — and be rid of these men forever. Good Lord, even she would be caught or killed eventually if she kept on living like this. No one was lucky forever. She had to convince them. "Listen to me. I'll go back to Colter. My account is still open at the bank so I have a legitimate reason for being there. I can check the place again and then drive out to your hideout and tell you if a guard came in that day. If not, I can go back and be stationed inside the bank when you come in."

"That'll make it pretty late in the mornin'," Bill said uneasily.

"It can't be helped," Margarita answered. "Unless you just want to ride straight in."

"We better wait for Margarita to let us know," Bert advised.

Openly Sam asked, "What about gettin' shot?"

51

Margarita reacted with an impatient toss of her head. "Don't be stupid, Sam. I'm telling you we can pull this off."

"Well," Bill said, and grinned at her through his rotten teeth. "You'll be the first to go, won't you, if the whole damn deal falls through?"

"I may be first down. But you might be second, so you had better be watching your own back." She glared unwaveringly at him while he stared back in return, finally turning his eyes away. He had better know she meant it.

"I'd better ride up to Wagon Mound and take the stage from there," she said thoughtfully. "I can't go by way of Dusty Springs again, they'll be looking for me for stealing that horse and buggy."

They spent more time discussing their timing. She would arrive in Colter a day ahead of the rest. They would ride straight to the hideaway.

"What'll we do with the horses we ride there?" Sam asked.

"Leave 'em," Bert said practically. "We won't have time to fool with 'em. We can always buy more."

"Or rustle 'em," Bill laughed.

Margarita said, "I have the place for you to hole up all picked out. It has plenty of water and grass and privacy. I'll draw you a map."

Bert had a worried look on his face. "I'd hate to die richer'n hell right there in Colter."

"You won't die, Bert. None of us will."

"Well, Margarita," he said warmly, and put an unusually friendly arm around her shoulders. "You've been right for the past two years. I'm with you."

* * * * *

52

Six days later, under heavily overcast skies, attired in her yellow dress, Margarita drove out of Colter in a rented buggy. At a brisk trot she headed toward the amphitheater where the men and horses were resting and waiting. As a place of refuge, it was ideally suited just three miles from town, the pasture land used only by grazing cattle. The valley floor, thick with grass, gave the horses plenty to eat, and a small stream fulfilled their need for water. Tall thick stands of pine and cedar growing against the walls of the amphitheater offered shade and shelter from sun and rain.

Margarita arrived shortly after nine-thirty, following the well worn path of cattle that wandered in and out of the area. The sky looked like rain today, a very good sign; the buggy's tracks, as well as the horses', would be badly smeared in a good downpour. If not, it didn't matter anyway. The gang wasn't returning here. Margarita had already selected a second place to hide after the robbery, if it was needed. She thought she had covered every avenue of escape, every possibility of danger. She felt confident that she had done her best, that everything was completely under control.

The men came from behind the trees on either side of the amphitheater's entrance as she rode in to meet them. Holstering a prudently drawn gun, Bert asked, "What'd you find out?"

"I was just in the bank. There is no guard. And only two tellers. Look for my buggy out front."

After a few more minutes of discussion, Margarita left, arriving in town shortly after ten. The others would be along at any moment. Bert would bring her horse with him, saddled and ready.

It would be hard to ride in a dress. The robbery would also finally identify this gang as having a woman member.

That couldn't be helped. It wouldn't matter anyway if her share was enough for her to pull out.

Drawing to a stop in front of the bank, she looked down the street and saw the men riding in. They would be here within the next minute.

Her heart thudding, she went inside and walked to the back of the bank. She began to rummage through her pouchlike purse as if trying to find some elusive object. The purse, made of knitted wool and hanging with thin drawstring handles from her wrist, was awkward to carry, concealing as it did her heavy gun. As she continued pawing at imaginary objects, Bert opened the door and walked in, followed closely by Sam and Bill.

Two other people were conducting business at the windows. She saw her partners glance quickly about, checking for themselves that she had been right about the guards. Apparently reassured, each man took a position at the windows, Bert and Sam behind the customers, Bill standing alone. Covering them from the rear, Margarita remained at the back wall beneath the mural, continuing to look through her purse.

They all waited with nervous impatience until the townspeople left. As soon as the door had closed, Bert drew his gun and said with a growl, "This is a stick-up." Bill and Sam had drawn their own revolvers. Margarita had her hand on hers, still hidden within the purse, but was now beginning to draw it out.

At Bert's words, both tellers simultaneously disappeared behind the counter, dropping to the floor with lightning speed.

Sam turned toward Bert. "What the hell —"

Margarita had tightened her hand around the gun inside her purse and had already cocked the hammer. But her grip froze on the butt of the pistol as a shot rang out.

In wide-eyed and unbelieving horror she watched blood explode from the back of Bert's head. He was dead before he hit the floor. Another bullet hit Bill high in the back as he and Sam raced for the door. A volley of shots followed them. The door slammed loudly behind the outlaws before Margarita could think or act. Neither man had had time to fire even once in return.

Margarita looked around to see where the shots had come from. There were still no guards visible.

"You all right, ma'am?" a muffled voice from above and behind the wall of the painting called to her.

A molten chunk of fear filled Margarita's stomach. She looked up at the picture. The benevolent faces of the man and his wife were gone. So was one of the faces of the children. In their places were small square hinged openings. From two of the openings protruded gun barrels.

My God, the painting! She had never even considered it: a cleverly built false wall. And the picture was nothing but a trick . . . a way to put watchmen high and out of sight on some type of platform. The guards must have been peeking through holes in the peoples' faces. A stranger would never know. Never guess.

Wisely, she eased the hammer of the gun home and slowly withdrew her hand from her purse, closing it tightly by its strings.

Heavy footsteps rapidly descended stairs she couldn't see. In a moment, two men came from a side door of the bank's interior. "You all right, ma'am?" asked a bearded young man in the same voice that had previously addressed her.

"I'm fine," she assured both guards, wiping a shaking hand across her face. Neither man seemed to have any idea that she was a part of this holdup.

In fact, she could walk away free. She could leave it all — and run! She could get out — right now! But could she? If she deserted the remaining gang, she would have to start all over again — find new people, tougher perhaps, than those with whom she now worked . . . just to protect herself, because Bill, if he lived, would come after her eventually, no doubt believing that she had betrayed them. And worse, she would have to rebuild her entire stake.

She wasn't one bit willing to give up two years work. She *must* attempt to set things straight.

"Are . . . are you going after them?" she asked in an unsteady voice.

It occurred to her that if the posse was lucky enough to catch Sam and Bill, then she wouldn't have to worry about them at all. Now or ever! Here or at the meadow. She would consider herself lucky to have lived through this and begin only with what she had right now — and be thankful it was that much. This failure had taught her in an instant that she had had enough of running outside the law.

"Wal, this here one's deader than cowshit," a grizzly bearded man pronounced as he unceremoniously rolled Bert over with the toe of his boot.

The tellers had come from behind the counter to stare at the lifeless man. "We get 'em every time, don't we?" commented one impassively.

Bert stared up at Margarita with unseeing eyes.

The second guard spoke with a smile. "Not this time. Afraid I got a little sloppy and missed that one fella. I bet his partner's gonna die, though." Calmly he refilled his gun, then whirled the barrel before sliding the weapon into its holster.

56

"I'll get the sheriff," a teller said. "There's probably a reward on him. Hope it's plenty."

Dead, Bert was finally worth money.

The first guard answered Margarita's question. "A posse will go after them. We'll catch them, too. Why don't you leave for now, ma'am?" he suggested. "Come back after we get this mess cleaned up. Shore sorry you had to see this."

Margarita smiled weakly, and wordlessly left the bank to climb shaking into the buggy. Her getaway horse still stood saddled and ready at the hitching post. The stallion nickered at her in recognition but she did not dare make a move toward him. She *hated* losing horses. It was no different than continuously losing faithful friends.

She looked toward the sheriff's office. Men were already gathering, forming a posse. She could at least ride over Sam and Bill's tracks with the buggy; it might confuse the law somewhat, and aid the men's escape. She might delay the posse a moment, too, with some flirtatious dupe. By then, riding like hell, the two fugitives should be miles away if they had any brains. She began her drive in the direction they had ridden.

She hadn't gone two miles when a cloudburst erupted — great thick, heavy drops of rain. She didn't want to take the time to stop the buggy to raise the top, but it wouldn't make sense when the posse finally reached her to find a strange woman openly riding in a downpour. It would surely raise unnecessary questions.

The top in place, rain landed with a slap on the thin, tough leather overhead and dripped from its swinging tassels, spraying Margarita unpleasantly. But she thanked God the deluge came when it had; it would help conceal tracks.

She had traveled only another quarter mile or so when Sam leaped from behind a large boulder, startling Margarita's horse. Hauling back on the reins, she struggled to bring the rearing animal to a standstill. Sam reached up and grabbed the bridle, assisting her. What in the world was he doing so close to town? When the gelding stood quietly, Sam walked to her side, rain dripping heavily from the brim of his hat, obscuring his face. "How's Bert?" he asked.

"Dead," Margarita answered. "He never had a chance. I came back to take the blame," she said, fighting a shaking voice.

"It's a bad deal, Margarita. How come you didn't see that paintin'? Bill said he's gonna kill you."

"I looked at everything, Sam. It just looked like a painting, nothing else."

Sam pursed his lips, studying her hard through the downpour.

"I'm sorry," she said. The words sounded stupid.

Sam grunted, whether in agreement or disagreement, Margarita couldn't tell. He said, "Come here and look at Bill. He's hurt real bad."

"Then you ought to forget Bill and get going," she advised. "The posse's coming."

"Look at him," he insisted as he half-dragged her behind the rock.

Bill lay on the ground, rain pounding his unprotected face. She knelt beside him. Pale and barely breathing, he rolled his head toward her. Only with great effort was he able to focus his eyes on her. Unsuccessfully, he tried to blink away the rain. "Get me some help, Margarita. I can make it. I know I can. Get the doc."

No death threats from him now. The man was finished. "This is no place to hide," she said, looking up at Sam. "You should ride."

"Bill wants help. He says he can make it." Sam stepped closer to her side.

"You're loco." She nearly laughed. "He's dying."

Quietly Sam said, "Not if he says he ain't dyin', and he says he ain't. You go on and get help. Meet us right here after dark. We gotta pull together."

Soaked with rain and chilled to the bone, he led her back to the buggy. She climbed into the seat.

Sam held his hand to the brim of his hat and looked down the road, squinting against the downpour. "I see 'em coming. You do somethin' to draw that posse off'n our trail."

He ducked behind the boulder as Margarita brought the reins down on the horse in a stinging blow, urging him into a dead gallop. She saw the lawmen gaining rapidly on her. Harder and harder she beat on the horse's rump, pressing him to run until his sides heaved. Just before the horsemen reached her, she released one rein and let it fly freely from the horse's bit and off to one side. She began to scream as if in mortal fear of her life — and realistically, she felt she was.

The four riders came galloping hard alongside the buggy, two on each side. The leaders grabbed for the bridle of the runaway with loud yells of "Whoa, whoaaa," until the men were finally able to stop the out-of-control animal. Seemingly shaken and panic-stricken, Margarita said breathlessly, "Thank goodness you came along." She leaned heavily and helplessly against the tall man who helped her from the buggy.

He asked, "What'er you doin' out here in the rain?"

Margarita panted, "I . . . I thought I could take a drive before it came. I . . . lost a rein. I didn't judge very well, did I?"

"No, ma'am, you didn't." A thin reed of a man walked over to her. "You'd best turn yourself around and head straight back to town. The bank was just held up and the bandits came this way not long ago."

"My God," she gasped and fainted in the mud at the men's feet.

She opened her eyes a few minutes later. Ponchos, one under her and one over her, protected her body. A hat held by one of the men shielded her face. All four deputies squatted at her side. "Here, ma'am," a bearded man offered, and held her head while she drank from his canteen.

Slowly she sat up. "I'll be fine now." Soaked and dirty, she wished she were dead.

"You better get on back to town," a deputy advised, helping her into the buggy. "It ain't safe out here."

"Yes, of course," she agreed. "I'm sorry to have delayed you."

She turned the vehicle around, thanking and thanking them, stalling . . . stalling . . . stalling, then headed back to Colter. Glancing back through the gloom, she saw two posse members studying the ground around them, checking for tracks in the muddy road while the remaining two mounted up.

Eventually they would figure out that Sam and Bill had spent time behind the boulder three quarters of a mile behind them, but she was sure her deliberate delay, and the rain that hadn't yet let up, had given the two outlaws more than enough time to ride as fast as they were able to manage to some place of safety. In the continuing heavy downpour their chances of escape increased with each passing minute.

With Bill more than half dead, Margarita could not imagine Sam wasting his time trying to drag the stricken outlaw along. She thought she understood men. Especially these men. She had been dead wrong.

She turned all thoughts to finding medical assistance' unnoticed assistance. Colter's doctor? Out of the question. He would turn her in at first opportunity — assuming she could get him to cooperate to begin with. And, no doubt, cooperation would have to be at gunpoint. Who then? The druggist? What was his name? Henry. Yes, she could probably bribe the druggist. It seemed that it would be much easier to buy off a druggist than to threaten a doctor.

She assumed the bribe would have to be plenty. She would enter the drugstore just before closing; invite him to her hotel room; entertain him until nightfall. If that wasn't enough, there was always money. Together they would ride to her partners. When Henry was finished fixing up Bill, she would have Sam get rid of him — and get her money back.

A little more than an hour after the ill-fated robbery attempt, Margarita was back in her room again. She had avoided the hotel clerk's questioning eyes as he looked at her disheveled appearance. "A tub of hot water immediately," she ordered as she breezed by. "And a delivery boy at once."

The boy arrived within five minutes and was sent to the women's apparel shop with an exact list of what Margarita wanted. He was to be back in one hour. No sooner.

During that hour, Margarita threw aside her filthy clothes and bathed. She could take no pleasure in the almost searing heat of the hot soapy water, only seeing Bill's fevered eyes as he lay on the ground looking up at her through the falling rain. Near death or not, a sense of mortal fear of the man overpowered her. She closed her eyes, trying to force her mind away from today's enormous problems.

Right on time came the expected knock on her door. Wrapped in a sheet, she let in an embarrassed young man loaded down with boxes. Hurriedly he set the packages on the bed and left.

Margarita waited until ten minutes to five before leaving the hotel. She looked striking now in a new bottle-green silk dress. Her hair, clean and striking, was carefully but loosely combed back, allowing it to catch the day's light in gentle waves. In a white woolen purse was concealed her gun. Thoughtlessly running a finger across her scar, she took no pleasure in her fresh appearance.

The rain had given way to warm rays of bright sunshine, and it took a moment for her eyes to adjust to the dim interior of the drugstore. With effort she called out cheerily, "Henry?"

"Back here," came a gravely voice. An old, old man rose from behind a counter near the rear of the store and came toward her. Completely bald, his face criss-crossed with hundreds of tiny lines, he had no teeth except for one near the front. A white shirt, held against his bony chest with suspenders, was spattered with tobacco stains from the day's attempts and misses at a spittoon somewhere out of Margarita's sight. He was bent with age.

"You're Henry?" Margarita asked incredulously. This was no one she could entertain until nightfall. She doubted he would last an hour. And he would never do to help Bill.

"And who might you be?" he asked, leaning heavily against the counter.

"A friend of a friend," she answered lightly. She didn't know what old Henry's role might be when someone brought a wounded victim into the store and the doctor was away, but doubted he was able to venture very far on his own. Even now he was shaking where he stood. No, he would never do.

As if to verify her observation, Henry said, "Guess I'll set a might," and shuffled unsteadily to the center of the store with the aid of a cane to ease himself down with a groan into the same chair the injured cowboy had occupied a couple of weeks before. "An' who's this here friend of yours?"

Margarita named the only person with whom she was even remotely acquainted. "Julia Blake." Even as she said it, the answer came like a flash of lightning. Julia could help Sam! Henry probably only directed Julia's movements whenever she tended an injured man.

Wonderfully, the old man's next words confirmed the fact. "Fine lady next to my wife, rest her soul," he said, looking at Margarita with puddly yellowed eyes. "Does everything around here from runnin' the place when I'm feelin' punk to fillin' in when the doc's out. She'll be along any minute if you wanna visit. Store'll be closin' soon." Henry opened his mouth and yawned widely, finishing with a "Ho, ho hum."

"Thank you," Margarita said, turning her back on the decrepit old man, thinking about the whole new life Julia Blake was about to begin.

Chapter Six

The bell tinkled overhead as Julia entered the
drugstore carrying a small package wrapped in brown
paper. "Here's your sandwich, Henry," she called out
cheerily, closing the door behind her and sending another
tinkle of sound throughout the quiet little store. She
glanced Margarita's way. "Why . . ."

"Old friend to see you, Julia," Henry announced, and
pointed a shaking bony finger at Margarita who had been
tensely browsing about the store while she waited.

"Goodness, I never dreamed of seeing you again." Julia spoke in tones of amazement.

Margarita nodded curtly. She became uneasy under Julia's openly studious gaze.

"Be with you in a minute," Julia said to her, and went to Henry's side. "Here, Henry. Enjoy your sandwich. Would you like your spittoon beside you?"

"Naw, jest bring me the small can, thank you. Wouldn't want a lady handlin' somethin' like that ol' brass mess."

Patting him affectionately on a thin shoulder, she gently chided him, "Now you know, Henry, that I clean that ol' brass mess every day. It's no trouble at all." She walked to the rear of the room and brought back the spittoon, setting it beside his chair.

Margarita had to work at speaking pleasantly. "I saw something in the window I liked. May I show you?" She led Julia to the store front in an attempt to get her as far from Henry as possible.

Both women bent slightly over the object Margarita had fixed her attention upon, a small mirror encased in a delicate silver stand.

Julia spoke softly — and coldly. "Two of your men were shot this morning. Is that why you're here?"

An overwhelming wave of fear washed over Margarita. How, in God's name, did this woman know that? *How?* No matter. She knew!

Margarita warned severely, "If you think anything of that old man back there, you'll do exactly as I say." Her hands shook violently as she nudged Julia slightly in the elbow with her purse.

Glancing down at the woolen bag, Julia nodded in understanding.

Margarita spoke quietly. "I need medical help — and I can't bring the doctor. You seem to know what to do. Tell the old man you're going on a trip. You won't be back for a few days." Bill was going to require her at least that long.

"That's a ridiculous reason," Julia answered bluntly. "I just got back from traveling, a few weeks ago — as you well know."

Margarita was aghast. Did this mean that the saleswoman even knew who had robbed her? It appeared so. But *how*? How did she know these things? Did she know who the rest of the gang was? Their names?

Sweat broke out in tiny beads on her forehead. Beneath her dress perspiration began to trickle down her sides. She was angry with herself for her fear and enraged with this Anglo for having caused that fear. She leaned close to the woman. "You do what I tell you, *señorita*. Tell Henry whatever you have to. Bring what you need to help my partner. If you don't obey, old Henry is *muerto*." She turned and faced him, her purse held menacingly before her.

Julia turned abruptly and walked over to her employer, kneeling by his side, Margarita following closely. "Henry, dear," Julia said, "This lady has invited me to visit. It's a few days drive from here. She's asked me to come so often that I feel guilty saying no to her once again. Maude can fill in for me."

"You jest got back," he protested.

"I know," Julia answered. "But it's an area of New Mexico I haven't seen."

"You gonna bring back new dust?"

"I hope so."

Margarita barely heard Henry's strange question. All she heard was the name Maude.

"Who's Maude?" she asked a little too sharply.

"His niece," Julia responded, standing. "She helps Henry when I can't." She addressed the old man again. "I'll just take some things along. Maude can lock up for you this evening."

"Go ahead," Henry agreed reluctantly.

Julia walked behind a counter with Margarita close by her side. There would be no hidden guns to trick her. Julia bent down and collected several drugs from a low shelf and put them into an already bulging black leather medical bag — a good sign for Bill that Julia probably doctored regularly when Colter's doctor was not available.

As she began to rise, Margarita put a firm hand on her shoulder. "You can't leave like that. The satchel's a dead giveaway. Do something. Fast! Make up some excuse."

Leaving the bag on the floor, Julia ripped brown paper from a large roll on the countertop. Squatting, she wrapped the bag, then bound it with heavy brown string. "I'll take some knickknacks with me," she called to Henry, "and try to sell some for you."

When he didn't respond, Margarita glanced his way. "He's asleep. Let's move."

"I must go get Maude first," Julia said.

"Where is she?"

"She lives about a mile outside of town."

Margarita could barely conceal her frustration at this new turn of events. Impatiently she said, "All right, damn it, let's get going. Where's your buggy?"

"Out back."

Margarita saw that she would need the hotel clerk to return her rig after she checked out. She could not just abandon it.

They left the medical bag in Margarita's room while she and Julia went for Henry's niece. Forty-five minutes later, Julia, Margarita, and a scarecrow of a woman with a prominent hook nose, entered the drugstore. All the way back to town Maude had bitched continuously that Julia had given her no notice. "The only time I ever see you, Julia," she had said in a constant shrill voice, "is when you need me to fill in for you. I ought to be working there full time and you well know it." The woman had nearly driven Margarita out of her mind.

Margarita stood just inside the doorway, listening to every word spoken as Julia made final arrangements with Maude and Henry before leaving.

The two women returned to the hotel to retrieve their belongings, Margarita keenly alert to any sign Julia might give to the desk clerk that she was in danger. But there was none.

Seated in the buggy once again, Julia leaned toward Margarita and inquired sarcastically, "And now, do you bind and gag me?"

Feeling that somehow she was being made fun of, Margarita replied through clenched teeth, "We leave Colter and hole up somewhere till nightfall."

Julia laughed mockingly. "Hole up? You *are* a bandit, aren't you? No one else would use such a silly expression." She laughed again.

Margarita felt a surge of anger at Julia's ridicule. She, Margarita, was doing the abducting, yet Julia seemed to be the one in control.

"I'm not sure I'm up to holing up," Julia acknowledged. "Why don't we just make life easy and simply wait at my place until dark?" She added, "I don't expect things are going to be the same again for a while."

Margarita noted with some satisfaction the tiredness in the tone. "Where is your place?"

"Back toward Maude's." Julia gestured with her head. "Not quite as far."

"Who else is there?"

"No one."

"Where's everyone else?"

"There is no one else. I live alone."

"Alone? Women don't live alone unless their man's gone."

"I do. My parents are both dead. And there is no man."

"Why?" Margarita pulled the buggy up in front of the hotel.

"Why not?"

Because, thought Margarita, women do not normally live independently. They are laughed at and thought of as odd — as old maids. Who wanted to die all alone? She would rather be shot or hung as a bandit. She said, "I don't believe you."

"You'll have to trust me. It would be more pleasant and just as safe as hiding in a ditch somewhere."

"We'll see."

Julia drove the buggy directly through the open doors of a small red barn. Margarita watched her unhitch the horse and put him in a stall. Julia rubbed him down while he munched on oats and hay and sucked thirstily from a bucket she had filled from a trough just outside the door. Margarita offered no help, not daring to be distracted even slightly.

Julia unlocked the rear door of a small two-story house surrounded by several piñon trees. The much cooler air that flowed from inside was almost a caress against Margarita's hot cheeks as she followed Julia through the doorway and into the kitchen. She noticed instantly the harmony within the house itself. This was a home where only one person could possibly live. It was far too neat. The dwelling was obviously decorated to please only one person's eye, but anyone looking at Julia's home would have been deeply charmed. Windows were decorated with soft green and blue curtains, with a matching tablecloth on a round table surrounded by four spindle backed chairs. Yellow flowers in a tall slender vase rested in the center of the table. Against a wall, china gleamed from the shelves of a red oak hutch. Canned goods were stacked neatly on shelves built into the walls. The stove looked freshly blackened, and a wide plank floor gleamed chalk white from countless scrubbings.

Julia walked through the kitchen and into the parlor, trailed by Margarita whose hand was still in her purse. Impatiently Julia turned on her. "Oh, put that damn thing away, Margarita. I'm not going anywhere until you tell me to, and no one is coming by that I know of. If they do, I'll take care of it. Now, relax."

Margarita said nothing but did remove her hand.

In the living room, Julia flopped into an over-stuffed chair near the door and wiped a slender hand across a light sheen of moisture on her brow. "Good lord, Margarita, do sit down." She spoke with exasperation. "I feel like you're going to shoot me at any moment." She closed her eyes and rested her head against the back of the chair.

Two big chairs and a large couch, each covered with the placid colors of large orange roses and green leaves, dominated most of the room. The use of such colors struck Margarita as odd but at the same time, sensible. Lanterns, their chimneys clean of soot, sat on small cherry tables near the couch and chairs. Overhead hung a five-lantern wagonwheel chandler suspended by link chains of silver. A fireplace of stone, clean of ashes, took up much of one wall. In front of the fireplace lay a thick, brightly printed carpet that sank beneath Margarita's feet. Two very well done paintings of mountains and streams hung on the walls. Margarita thought briefly of her own dingy dwelling; she did not long dare compare their two homes.

She drew her attention back to her prisoner. Surprisingly, Julia had dozed off; her head lolled slightly to one side, and she snored very gently. How could she possibly sleep at a time like this?

Margarita stared at her and at a tan throat exposed by the white opened-neck dress of linen. She studied the soft skin of Julia's cheeks, and the red lips — lips more scarlet than normal, sensuous lips that would fill a man with passion. Again Margarita wondered about this woman. Any lady as beautiful as she was had a man. Why did Julia Blake not conform to this rule?

Julia's fingers dangled over the edge of the chair. Once in a while she would twitch in her sleep. Without explanation, Margarita wanted to take her in her arms and comfort her seeming vulnerability.

She waited patiently until her captive awoke an hour later. Margarita's first words were: "We'll have to ride double on your horse. Wear long underwear and pants and a warm shirt and coat. And heavy boots. A hat, too. It gets cold traveling at night. Do you have such clothes?"

"I do," Julia answered briefly. "My father's."

Just before dark, they changed to men's attire. It was a relief to Margarita to put on her riding clothes even though they were dusty and dirty from previous wearings and being crammed for days into a small suitcase. She felt even better when she wrapped her gunbelt around her waist.

71

Margarita had Julia pack enough provisions for themselves and Sam and Bill, for the return journey to the meadow. They would have to eat sparingly, but they would make it.

They walked out to the barn where, by a single lantern, Julia saddled the horse and then led him outside. She bolted the door behind her as she had the house. A quick glance around the place by lantern light seemed to satisfy her that everything was in order.

Margarita tied the medicine bag and a cold lantern freshly filled with kerosene behind the saddle, securing them tightly with leather thongs. The saddlebags were already crammed with her dress, shoes, and food.

It was time to ride.

Julia doused the lantern and left it to cool beside the back door of the kitchen. She mounted up, then removed her foot from the stirrup so that Margarita could climb up behind her.

As the women made their way past the house and onto the road, clouds completely hid the stars and moon. They rode steadily for ten minutes when suddenly Margarita said, "Someone's coming. Hold up." She wrapped an arm tightly around Julia's waist as she listened, pulling the woman hard against her chest. She reached for her gun with her free hand. "Pull off." Her grip tightened even further. In the darkness, Julia guided the horse out of sight behind a clump of trees.

"Not a sound," Margarita warned softly. A whiff of Julia's perfume assailed her. She drove the scent from her consciousness.

As the riders drew nearly abreast of them, Margarita could tell by the sound of the horses' hooves that there were only four. So Bill and Sam had gotten safely away. They had been too long on the trail to be outwitted by an occasional town posse chasing after badmen, and, too, the rain had been an immense help.

The women sat for another few minutes before moving. Self-consciously Margarita discovered she still had her arm around Julia, and let go.

Another ten minutes of easy riding brought them near the rock where Sam had stopped her this morning. "Slow down," Margarita ordered, and Julia pulled back slightly on the reins. They traveled another few paces before Margarita had her stop altogether. They waited in the road. Their mount snorted once, the jingling of his harness the only other sound to be heard. Margarita listened to her own breathing, none too steady. Sam was out there right now, probably with drawn gun, checking to make sure that it was she and the doctor — and no one else.

Finally out of the darkness he spoke. "Over here."

Even though she was expecting him, his voice made her jump. Both she and Julia dismounted at once.

Margarita untied the medicine bag, then handed it to Julia while Sam lit the lantern, turning the wick only high enough to guide them and the horse behind the rock.

"How is he?" Margarita asked, squatting down beside the wounded man. Again Bill lay on the ground, this time face down. He moaned his intense pain. Beneath him was a poncho and, covering him, a blanket.

Sam lifted the lantern. "Can you fix 'im, Doc?" He glanced at Julia as the light danced off her eyes. "What the hell . . . This is a woman! What's she doin' here?"

"There is no doctor, Sam," Margarita pronounced. "Just her. So move out of the way so she can get to work."

He cursed, then spat on the ground. "No damn female is doctorin' a man."

"Then shoot Bill right now and be done with it," Margarita snapped. "Because if you don't let her tend him, he's going to die. There was no doctor in town."

Sam hesitated, then stepped aside, still cursing. Julia immediately knelt beside the prostrate outlaw. "Where is he hit?" she asked.

"His back. Shot in the back by some coward," Sam snarled.

In the light of the lantern, Margarita could see Julia stiffen. But she did not comment. She asked for more light, and the lantern was placed by her side and turned up slightly. "Hold the light up," she said. Margarita picked up the lantern, bringing it close to Sam's back.

Pulling back the blanket, then tearing the bloody shirt away, Julia exposed the wound. The bullet had entered the right shoulder muscle. She touched the area near the puncture. Bill let out a low scream.

"If the bullet isn't taken out right away, he'll die of blood poisoning. Gag him. Margarita, open that bag and give me a bottle of alcohol."

In seconds, the bottle was in Julia's hand. Sam tied his bandanna firmly around the injured man's mouth.

"Hold him tight," she said to her two assistants. Margarita set the lantern down beside Julia.

"If he dies . . ." Sam warned.

"Shut up, Sam," Margarita barked. "If he dies, blame me. Leave her out of it."

"Both of you shut up," Julia ordered. "Hold him. He's going to fight now." Without warning she poured alcohol over the bullet hole. Bill struggled wildly, half mad with pain. Pouring more alcohol over a pair of large tweezers, she began to dig into his back. He fought them all for another minute and then lay still.

"You killed him," Sam bawled.

"He's just fainted," Julia replied. "Margarita, hold that lantern up. I need to hurry."

Julia dug deeper and deeper into the unconscious man. It seemed to Margarita that Julia's probing must penetrate Bill's chest before she stopped. Blood poured freely from the wound.

"Sam," Julia instructed, "pour more alcohol onto his back." In another minute Julia pulled from Bill the bullet that had stopped halfway through his chest.

"He'll have to be bound tightly and not be moved for several days," Julia pronounced, efficiently moving from one task to another. "Sit him up."

Together Margarita and Sam held Bill in position while Julia wrapped clean strips of cloth round and round his back and chest.

The now half-conscious outlaw began to moan as Julia finished bandaging him. It took all three to get Bill into a coat.

"Come on, Margarita," Sam said. "Help me get him in my saddle. We'll take turns tyin' him against us. I'll go first. What's the soonest we can reach the hideout?"

"At least three days riding like hell," she replied.

"I told you," Julia declared firmly. "He can't be moved. He needs a bed right now or he'll likely die."

Sam walked over to Julia and picked up the lantern, holding it close to her face as Margarita steadied Bill in the saddle. "Oh,no ne won't lady. Because you're gonna make sure he don't."

As Sam tied Bill against his own body for the return ride to the meadow, the women gathered the medicine bag's contents together. Then Sam said sternly, "Margarita, blindfold that woman."

She glanced Julia's way and then toward Sam. "Blindfold her? She can't ride hard like that."

"Wal, she's gonna." He drew his gun and pointed it at Julia.

"I won't do it!" Margarita declared hotly. She had done enough to Julia Blake already.

The click of a hammer being drawn back broke the sound of the still night air.

"It's all right, Margarita," Julia said, coming to her side. "Here, use this." She handed Margarita a strip of cloth and removed her hat.

Margarita gently but firmly wrapped the cloth around her captive's eyes, tying it behind her head. "Are you all right?" she whispered. There was a barely discernible nod from Julia. Margarita led her to her horse, assisted her in mounting, guiding her foot into the stirrup and her hand onto the pommel. Once she was in the saddle, Margarita took the reins of Julia's horse and walked over to Bill's mount.

"Tie her hands, too," Sam ordered.

"Like hell I —"

"Do it!"

Margarita obeyed. Sam was nervous as a cat. She could not challenge him now regardless of how she felt about the way Julia was being treated. She had no one to blame but herself.

With no further time for thought, she secured the medicine bag to the back of the horse, mounted up, and, leading Julia's horse by the reins, began to follow Sam.

They rode steadily and rapidly through the night, pausing twice only to let their horses drink from a small stream. The following dawn, they traveled along the arroyos and creeks and through canyons that Margarita hadn't even known existed in this area.

Around noon, Sam called a halt beside a flowing stream dense with brush and near the entrance of a craggy canyon. "I gotta take a leak."

Margarita turned to see if Julia had heard his crude words. If she had, she gave no indication. Since last night she had not made a sound . . . had not complained. Margarita knew that old Henry was on her mind. Damn good thing, too. It kept her from doing something stupid. Margarita wouldn't have hurt Henry, but Sam might hurt Julia if she misbehaved.

Together Sam and Margarita untied Bill from Sam's waist and lowered him to the ground in the shade of a piñon tree. He was out cold. After removing his coat, they saw that his bandage was soaked through with blood.

"Turn her loose and let her work on him," Sam said, glancing in Julia's direction. "If she tries to escape, hobble her."

Free of the rope, Julia rubbed life back into her wrists before removing her blindfold. She dismounted and looked around at her surroundings. She seemed to be examining them so intently that Margarita wondered if she was trying to recognize landmarks.

Margarita untied the medicine bag and placed it at the unconscious man's side. Julia continued to rub her wrists as she knelt beside him. She spoke her first words since last night: "He's lost an awful lot of blood. I don't know if he'll make it."

"He'll make it." Sam stood right behind them.

She did not comment again as she unwound the bloody bandage, poured more alcohol on the wound, and then rewrapped it.

Sam sat down beneath the tree. "Bind her, Margarita."

"Why don't you just shoot us, Sam. We have things we have to do and we can't have our hands tied to do it."

"Two minutes an' I'll be lookin' for her." He drew his gun and waved it threateningly back and forth before both their faces.

Margarita took Julia by the arm and led her to a private area, leaving her alone while she went to relieve herself. But not trusting that Sam wouldn't come after them, both women were back within the short length of time he had allowed them. He was still jumpy and nervous and Margarita saw no point in worsening the situation.

They rested for a half hour. Sam wandered away, leaving Margarita to watch Julia, but still he remained within sight of them both.

The women sat on the ground, knees propped up, resting against a jutting rock along the stream. After hours of silence except for the brief reference to Bill, Julia spoke directly to Margarita. "There's your partner." The words sounded bitter.

Margarita looked in the direction of thick shrubbery where Julia had pointed.

"See that little bird flitting around?" Julia continued watching the shrubbery.

Margarita heard a *whichity-whichity-whichity-which* sound coming from a bushy area fifteen feet away. "I don't see anything."

"Wait."

Another minute passed before the bird landed on a slim twig long enough for her to see what Julia had been watching all along. "Oh, look. He looks like a little . . ."

". . . bandit," Julia finished for her. "He's called a yellowthroat. The place is crawling with desperadoes."

Margarita stared with fascination at the small bird. Olive green above, bright yellow below, fading into dull white on his belly, with a very distinct black mask predominant across his eyes, he did indeed look very much like a little bandit.

Margarita said, "I never paid much attention to birds. I don't think I've ever noticed this one before."

They watched the tiny creature fly into and around the brush until Sam announced that it was time to go. Refusing to give in to the stiffness of too many hours in the saddle, Margarita rose soundlessly. Julia, too, kept her silence, earning unspoken praise from Margarita as she bound her and restored the blindfold.

This time Bill was tied to Margarita's chest. Again Sam led the way.

They stopped twice more in the next day and a half, Margarita not recognizing where they were. After all she and the men had been through together, they still hadn't let her in on all the ways possible to and from the meadow. She was still a woman — and not to be trusted completely.

They reached the meadow within the three days Margarita had predicted, with their horses' tongues nearly hanging out before they finally stopped in front of the men's cabin. Julia had been kept blindfolded and tied the entire trip except when she had tended Bill or eaten. Remarkably, Bill still lived, slipping continuously in and out of consciousness.

Sam and Margarita clumsily carried him inside and laid him on a cot. Released to work on him, Julia looked down on him and hopelessly shook her head.

Julia's wrists were worn raw from having been bound for so many days and nights by the abrasive rope. But never once had she complained. Not used to riding a horse, she was sore to the point of limping badly, but neither did she complain when she walked. On the insides of her thighs and calves, spots of blood showed through her pant legs where the leather of the saddle had rubbed her skin raw.

Both Margarita and Sam watched closely as Julia tended Bill, her brows knitting fiercely as she grimaced in her own personal discomfort.

When she finished, Sam said, "Julia'll stay in here."

Surprising both Sam and Margarita, the saddle-weary woman whirled on Sam. Her voice was severe. "I will *not* stay in this filthy shack. I will come several times, day and night, to look at your wounded friend. But he does not need someone to stand over him watching his chest rise and fall. You can do that if you want to. I need to rest. My work with this man is done for now. Margarita, where do you stay?"

Margarita felt her heart clog her chest, heavy thumps crashing against her rib cage as she watched Julia stand up to Sam. No man in his right mind talked to him that way. Would he take it from a woman, someone he didn't trust to begin with?

His mouth drew into a vicious snarl as his hand curled clawlike near the butt of his pistol. He stood frozen and poised, looking first at Julia, who glared right back at him, and then at Margarita, who prayed he would not do something insane.

"For Bill's sake, Sam, for mine, keep your head." Margarita stepped between him and Julia.

Roughly, he brushed her aside, his eyes cold as ice. After what seemed an eternity, Margarita saw his fingers relax slightly, then his hand drop to his side. She breathed an internal sigh of relief.

"Tie her up an' get her outta here," he growled savagely. "Then let me sleep. I'm going nuts with you bitches."

"Look at her wrists, Sam," Margarita bravely argued. "They're becoming infected. She's not going to be able to help Bill at all if she's not allowed to take care of herself first."

"Tie 'er!" he screamed, and rubbed a dirty hand across his face. "Then get out!"

Julia was hastily bound. Together the women left the cabin with the sound of Sam uncorking a bottle and hurling curses after them.

"Maybe he'll drink himself into a stupor," Julia suggested hopefully as they hastened away.

"Not a chance," Margarita replied. "He can drink three of those bottles dry and not even stumble."

Arriving at the cabin, Margarita released Julia to tend to her wounds, then left long enough to fetch a bucket of water. She returned to find that Julia had removed her hot, sticky clothing and now lay nude on the cot. She was sweating heavily and already sleeping soundly. Margarita quietly set the bucket on the floor and walked over to her to look down on the worn woman.

Julia was so beautiful she nearly took Margarita's breath away. Creamy breasts jutted forward, resting ever so slightly to the side, looking as pliant as fresh bread dough. Her dark nipples were soft and relaxed. It was an effort for Margarita not to reach down and caress that softness. The triangle patch between Julia's thighs was as blond as the hair on her head, softly curling downward toward slim, strong thighs, slightly spread with one knee a little bent.

Margarita absorbed the sleeping Julia with thirsty eyes. She wanted to . . . to. . . . She could not identify her longing. There was something she yearned to do, and the way she felt and what she was thinking as she continued to stare at Julia's body was alien to her.

She forced her eyes away and, instead of waking Julia to dress her wounds, sat at the table and rested her head on her arms.

She woke an hour later, her neck cramped and her arms stiff from cradling her head. She sat up and stretched.

Julia was still asleep. Deciding not to disturb her, Margarita placed a stool beside the cot and quietly opened the medicine bag. She would tend Julia's wounds herself, letting her sleep until it was time to go.

She found the salve and smeared a light coating of the soothing jelly, first to Julia's wrists, then to the insides of her calves where the outer layer of skin had been completely worn away. Even as Margarita applied the salve, Julia did not stir, not even aware of her pain. Margarita scooped up another fingerful and began to rub it onto the wounds of her thighs. Julia's skin was as Margarita had thought it would be — soft, tantalizing. She finished one leg to begin the other. She didn't have to take this long to tend Julia. But she made herself believe that she did.

Julia stirred, opening her eyes slowly, to find Margarita caressing her thigh. "What are you doing?"

Margarita jumped guiltily. "Dressing your wounds," she pronounced too loudly. Red-cheeked, she pulled her hand away. "You can finish now. There still needs to be bandages added."

"You do it," Julia said. She smiled reassuringly and reached to place a hand on Margarita's knee. She closed her eyes and in seconds was asleep again.

Margarita sat motionless, hardly having heard Julia's words, staring at the slender hand still resting on her knee. She would never allow another woman to touch her this way. Her guilt made her realize what her own

82

intention had been. She had been touching the woman sexually. *Sexually!* She had realized it the moment Julia had asked what she was doing. Margarita could feel her face searing with embarrassment. She had been after Julia the way men go after women.

No, damn it, she had not! Her touch had been soft, gentle, not pinching and grabbing the way she had been grabbed dozens of times by men. She had been very kind with Julia. Men hurried. She hadn't hurried!

What are you saying, she asked silently. Why are you making these ridiculous comparisons? Her thighs ached. Her belly ached. She wanted to run . . . run from Julia, from Sam, from the meadow . . . from herself.

Rapidly and with trembling fingers she finished nursing Julia's wounds, then carefully removed the exhausted woman's hand from her thigh. Knowing that to linger was to become entangled in something she knew nothing about, she snapped the medicine bag closed, and hurried outside.

A half hour later she awakened Julia who immediately rose and dressed. Even though Julia's wrists were still swollen, Margarita loosely retied her hands to pacify Sam.

"How about your legs, Julia?" Margarita asked. "How do they feel? I know you hurt."

"I'm certainly not as tough as I once thought I was," Julia admitted, "but I'll be fine."

Margarita released Julia to re-dress Bill's wounds. The area around the bullet hole was white with pus and had begun to smell. "We'll have to take turns watching him tonight," Julia said. "By then he'll be babbling nonsense. He's almost there now. Why he's still alive, I don't know."

Margarita felt a tremor of fear. Julia couldn't be allowed to listen to an outlaw's ravings; there was no telling what might be revealed. Julia already knew too much, and it was evident that Sam thought the same thing.

"Sam and I will spell each other, Julia." Margarita spoke hastily. "You sleep tonight. Tell us what to do."

Slumped forward on a stool, his elbows resting on the table, Sam nodded confirmation. Smoke from a cigarette held between his tobacco stained fingers curled toward the ceiling. "Tie Julia to your bed tonight, Margarita," he commanded.

Margarita saw Julia pause ever so briefly as she placed clean packing against Bill's back. Margarita cast unbelieving eyes toward Sam. "You're crazier than a damn coyote. You had her tied and blindfolded for three days. You're going to kill her, the way you're treating her. I'm warning you, Sam, if she doesn't show up back in Colter eventually, there will be a posse after us because they'll search until they find her. And you can bet your ass they'll find us, too. Don't ruin things now." She stood before him, fists clenched, fighting the desire to attack him and beat him senseless.

"Then she's gonna sleep in here. An' one word about anything Bill might let slip —"

In savage anger, Margarita slapped the table top with both palms. "All *right!* She sleeps in here. But so do I. So do we all. And damn it, forget about what Bill might say. Who the hell cares now, anyway?" Sam would not harm this woman. Would not!

Julia had completed her task and now stood at the bedside closing the medicine bag, not reacting to her two captors at all. When she had fastened the final strap, Sam rose and stepped to her side. He took hold of her wrist. Julia bit her lower lip to keep from crying out.

Margarita watched sharp-eyed as he picked up from the table a piece of rope. He was going to bind her hands together — again! It was obvious that he was planning to keep her tied all the time.

Margarita's very core rebelled — unexpectedly, violently — against Sam's endless sadistic actions of the past few days, his bossiness, his crudeness — what he was about to do now. Red spots appeared before her eyes. She felt dizzy and sick. She hated the man, hated his authority over her and Julia.

With a cry of outrage she grabbed a whiskey bottle and with a mighty swing smashed it against the edge of the table. Chunks and splinters of glass flew everywhere; the strong pungent odor of whiskey filled the room. Margarita clenched the jagged neck of the bottle and held it against Bill's throat, his skin dimpling beneath its pressure. Margarita shook with vehemence as she said, "Julia will not be kept tied like an animal, you bastard. And by God, we will not sleep in here — ever!"

Sam looked contemptuously at her from beneath his heavy lidded eyes. Unconcerned, he continued to wind the rope around Julia's wrists, smoke from his dangling cigarette floating lazily past his eyes.

Without mercy, Margarita pushed the bottle deep enough into Bill's neck to cut the skin. A trickle of blood ran down the side of his throat and onto the matted pillow.

Sam jumped forward. "Why you —"

She drove the bottle still deeper. Blood began to ooze more rapidly and thickly. "I'll slit his stinking throat, Sam," she warned.

Sam yanked the rope from Julia's wrists and slung it to the floor. "There, damn you!" he roared. "You'd best see she behaves."

Margarita turned to Julia. "Patch up Bill," she commanded, and cast aside the bottle neck. Without another word she stormed out of the cabin leaving Sam to clean up the mess and Julia to return on her own. If there was an outcry from Julia, Margarita would come to her aid instantly, gun drawn.

Alone in her cabin, she sat at the table and pounded her fists ' against the rough wood in blinding disappointment that the posse had failed to catch the men, that the guards hadn't shot all three of them dead in the bank, that she had forced Julia to come here.

"*Damn* it!" she uttered. A shadow fell across the threshold. She whirled, expecting Sam. "Oh, God," she sobbed when she saw Julia looking pale and shaken. "I *hate* you Anglos," Margarita cried loudly. "I hate *all* of you." She buried her face in her arms on the table, crying uncontrollably and feeling utterly defeated. What, in God's holy name, had happened to the peace she had once known in her life?

Julia walked over to Margarita and drew her to her feet. Gently, she pulled her close. "Shhh, Yellowthroat," whispered the taller woman into hair black as midnight.

The warmth of Julia's breath made Margarita's skin prickle. Feeling foolish at being held like a child, she began to pull away. Why the hell should Julia care about her? But Julia held firm, and Margarita soon yielded, wrapped warmly in Julia's arms. Julia murmured meaningless words into her ear and rubbed a strong, soothing hand up and down her back and stroked her hair and neck.

When Margarita finally managed to stop quaking, Julia released her. "Why are you so kind to me, Julia?" Margarita asked. She wiped away tears with the back of her hand.

"I don't know. I guess because you keep sticking up for me against your friend."

"But you're our prisoner — my prisoner."

"Don't think for a moment I've forgotten." Julia frowned deeply and sat on the cot. She began to pick at the woolen blanket covering the bed. "What you've done to me is stupid and cruel. I'll do what I can for Bill because no matter who I patch up, I try to give them my all. But then what? What happens to me after he recovers — or dies? Why should I allow myself to be consumed by hatred toward you? Toward them?" Julia tossed her head in the direction of the men's cabin. "It's a waste of time. I may not have a lot of time left. I'm not senseless enough to think I'm likely to get out of this."

Margarita turned to look at the pale woman seated on her cot. Julia was so different from her. Not be consumed by anger? By hatred? Had she run into someone stronger than herself?

Breaking into Margarita's thoughts, Julia asked, "Why do you stay here? You could change your life. You're not like the men."

Margarita walked to the doorway. With a sigh, she leaned against its edge. She might not be like the men but still she could not go; not with Bill hating her so. "If Bill lives he'll come looking for me. There's nowhere I could hide from him." She gazed out over the meadow with unblinking eyes. "I know he thinks I failed them all. But I checked that place a half dozen times. There was never a guard there. Only the tellers." Impatiently she wiped tears from her cheeks. "Who would ever suspect the painting was nothing but a trick? I never saw such a thing before. If I knew who was responsible, so help me God I'd shoot him dead."

She glanced at Julia, who sat rigid and white. "I'm sorry," Margarita apologized quickly. "I didn't mean to frighten you. Truthfully, I've never shot anyone. It's just that I feel so defeated sometimes."

Stammering, Julia replied, "It's . . . it's all right."

No it wasn't all right. Nothing was right. Hell, she didn't need to be reminded of her hopeless situation. She whirled on Julia in a sudden, new-felt wave of frustration. "What do you know, Anglo? Living in a fancy town. Wearing fancy dresses all the time. Look at your hands. Look at them!" Margarita walked to Julia and grabbed a hand, turning it palm upward. "Not a callous," she accused. "Not a scar. Soft as mash. Your hands are useless. You've never worked a day in your life! Don't tell me I should leave here." She added churlishly, "I have more money than you'll ever have just because I've stayed." She thrust Julia's hand from her own, a distasteful object, not to be touched.

"How dare you even say such a thing, Margarita Sanchez." Julia spoke incredulously. She pointed an accusing finger, her eyes blazing with anger. "You have everyone else's money. You have some of mine. You have none of your own."

Margarita exclaimed bitterly, "But I did have. Land, animals, a home. It was taken. All of it. In a moment — seven years of work — gone! Gone to Anglos. Jealous, greedy, stinking Anglos!"

She grabbed her hat and stalked out of the cabin. Julia had to step aside to avoid being pushed out of her path.

Margarita headed up the trail toward the pool. She would take a swim to cool off.

Damn it! She was so tired, hungry, worn down. She had never felt this way before. She knew she should rest. She couldn't even think straight anymore.

It pained her that she had yelled at Julia. But she had been unable to stop herself. The words had poured out uncontrollably. She had never even told the men as much as she had just revealed to this stranger. And she never knew she hated running with outlaws so much until she had lashed out at this innocent woman, taking out on her prisoner her inability to do something better with her own life.

Carelessly casting aside her hat she stripped to the skin, wishing she had brought along a fresh change of clothing. She should have brought Julia along, too. But the woman had sounded so damned righteous. Leaving her alone with Sam was stupid, but Margarita could think of nothing but escaping for a while. In any case, should their prisoner be in any kind of trouble, Margarita was sure Julia would scream her head off for help. And she, Margarita, could fight naked as well as clothed.

In another minute she was swimming on the bottom of the pool, gritting her teeth not against the cold water, but against her feelings about the kind of life she had been leading.

Chapter Seven

It was dark when Margarita awoke. Completely nude, she lay face down on top of a slab of rock, her hands tucked beneath her face to protect it. The moon hung low in the sky and stars twinkled brilliantly overhead. The mountain air was cool and penetrating.

She had just stood to dress when she heard a twig snap. Quickly, she ducked out of sight behind the rock. She hadn't brought her gun. Here at the meadow, she wasn't supposed to need one. Gone completely, she realized, was all the trust, however meager it may have been, that she and the gang had once shared.

With relief she watched the big papery moon silhouette Julia from behind as the panting woman climbed the last few feet of the path without benefit of lantern light. It was a wonder she hadn't sprained an ankle.

"That's a hell of a steep climb," Julia gasped, trying to catch her breath. "I'm not used to so much physical activity. Here, I thought you'd like a towel and soap."

Shyly Margarita came out from behind the rock, grateful for what little darkness there was. "How did you know where I was?" she asked. She took the towel Julia held out to her and, loosely folding it around herself, began to scrub away the tiny stones that had embedded themselves into her chest, belly, and thighs while she had slept.

"Sam came looking for you. He told me where you'd be. He said you're to take the next watch."

"When?"

"He didn't say. In an hour, I'd guess."

"How's Bill?"

"He's talking to himself and restless, but Sam's staying right with him."

"It's amazing Sam even gives a damn."

"Bill saved his life once."

Margarita looked up in surprise. "That must have been before we rode together. How did you learn that?"

"Bill began to mumble about it. Sam filled me in; says he owes Bill one. He's drunk," Julia added.

Margarita gave a snort of disgust. "He talks a lot when he's drunk. Are you all right?"

"I'm fine," Julia answered tiredly, and sat on a rock to rest.

In the pale light Margarita saw the shadow of a smile cross Julia's face. She said, "Bandits live terribly and argue among themselves a lot."

"They're frightening, too," Julia admitted. "Am I going to be shot?"

"No, Julia, you're not going to be shot. But I don't know when you're going home, either."

Julia let out a long sigh. Margarita heard her whisper, "Damn."

Impulsively she asked the downcast woman, "Would you like to go for a swim? The water is wonderful." The towel hung forgotten in her hands. And gone was the overwhelming anger she had earlier felt for Julia. This wasn't just another Anglo, another greedy Americano. This was Julia — resilient Julia — who had yet to complain about her circumstances.

"I don't know how to swim," Julia answered.

"That's all right. It isn't deep on this side. You can walk right along here for ten or twelve feet." Margarita indicated the area with a sweeping arm.

"I don't know . . ." Julia's voice trailed off.

"Come on," Margarita encouraged. "You'll sleep better."

"In these hovels? How do you people stand it?"

"My hovel is cleaner than the men's," Margarita replied with a smile.

Forgetting her nudity, she tossed the towel onto a rock and walked over to Julia and drew her to her feet by her elbows. Soon she was carefully leading her, naked and shivering, down over small rocks and into the water.

"Brrr, it's cold," Julia remarked with a shaking voice. She wrapped her arms tightly about herself.

"You'll get used to it. The water feels warmer at night. Just hang onto the edge. You'll be all right."

"I've never done this before." Julia's teeth chattered loudly. "It's not much like a hot tub in the kitchen, is it?"

"Not at all. It's a lot more fun. More freedom." Instantly Margarita regretted her words. "Take the soap," she said quickly, placing it carefully in Julia's hand. If she dropped it, she'd have a devil of a time finding it.

Julia splashed water on herself, gasping with each scoop, then slowly, almost sensuously, she began to rub the bar up and down her long slender arms and across her chest. Her pale, soapy skin glistened in the silvery light. It was difficult for Margarita not to stare at the taller woman, at the firm breasts thrust forward, the nipples erect, the body tense with chill.

She forced her eyes away from the intriguing and lovely vision, to swim to the center of the pool. Splashing water about, she announced, "Ahhh, this is great," and slid from Julia's sight.

When she broke surface, Julia was frantically calling her name, reaching out toward the center of the pool as far as she could with one hand while clinging desperately to the edge with the other. "Oh, my God, I thought you'd drowned!" The bar of soap was gone.

"No, *bobo*, I do this all the time."

"You put your head all the way under the water?"

"Yes, watch." Again Margarita was out of sight. In the inky blackness of the pool, she swam to Julia and with both hands grabbed her by the waist and burst upward through the surface, only inches from her face. Julia shrieked with fear.

Margarita threw back her head and laughed uproariously, delighting in teasing her, feeling devilishly carefree. "Here, you do it," she invited.

"Do what?"

"Take a deep breath and put your head under the water."

"You're addled. I'll die."

"You won't die. I won't let you."

Beneath the moon and stars the two women studied each other. Margarita could see the debate racing through Julia's mind. Should she trust her or not?

"You are the one Americano I like, Julia," Margarita assured her, attempting to put Julia at ease. "I won't drown you. I promise."

Julia clutched Margarita's forearms. "All right, I'll try."

Holding on with a claw-like grip that bit into Margarita's arms, Julia bent over and put her face into the water. In less than two seconds she came up gasping for air.

"Didn't you take a deep breath?" Margarita asked.

"Yes, but I didn't know how long I could hold it. I'll try once more."

Well, the lady had plenty of courage. But Margarita already knew that.

This time Julia squatted down and ducked completely under the water. She stayed only long enough to become totally submerged before jumping back up, but she had succeeded. With childlike delight, she squealed, "I did it!"

They laughed loudly, Margarita allowing Julia to hold her arms in bondage until both women had ducked beneath the water's surface several times, their knees banging together, and each time Julia coming up breathless and breathing loudly and deeply through wide-opened mouth.

"There, that's all there is to it. Now, when you paddle," Margarita advised, "you'll swim. Kick your feet, too."

"Not tonight," Julia gasped. "It must be near time to see to Bill again. I wouldn't want Sam to come up here."

In an instant, the lighthearted mood they shared was gone. The unpleasantness of her situation struck Margarita with the heaviness of a stone cast into the pool's serene water.

Too soon, the women were re-dressed in their sweaty, dusty clothing. Cautiously they made their way down the rocky slope, aided only by moonlight.

Julia asked, "What will Sam do if Bill dies?"

"He'll be angry," Margarita replied. She could almost feel the tension building around Julia. "He's not like this normally. But what the hell is normal anymore?" She felt it necessary to add: "Don't worry. I'll get you safely out of here."

To Margarita's surprise, Julia wordlessly took her hand and held it the rest of the way down the trail.

Margarita didn't let go until they reached the cabin.

Nor did she want to.

Chapter Eight

Bill grew worse and worse. There were days and nights when he would scream in agony, sometimes having to be held face down by his three attendants almost brutally so that he would not tear his bandages loose and rip open his wound. He raved, completely out of his mind as fever racked his body. Julia stayed with him constantly, fighting valiantly for his life, sitting long hours by his side both day and night. But in spite of her efforts, late in the afternoon eight days after he had been shot, he took a final breath, and died.

Julia looked up from the side of his cot where she had been kneeling. Sam stood beside her. "I tried, Sam. I really tried."

To Margarita it was touching the way Sam put his big hand on her shoulder. He sighed deeply and pursed his lips. "I believe you did, Julia. You're a good doctor. At first I thought you'd let him die on purpose. I didn't trust you. But, yeah, I think you did try."

Julia rose, and in gentlemanly fashion Sam offered her a stool, showing a side of himself that Margarita hadn't seen before. The three sat quietly together not speaking.

Finally Sam said, "I gotta ask, Julia. Why'd you try so hard?"

"He's a human being, Sam," she answered. "I treat all people the same, the drunks that are brought to me, the injured children, the innocent people who've gotten themselves shot." She glanced at the body of Bill, covered now with a blanket Margarita had placed over him.

Sam studied Julia for a long time before turning his eyes away. "Well, he run a good race. He was too damn crazy to live long, anyway."

"He was scum," Margarita said flatly.

"No denyin' it," Sam concurred. "All the same, I'm gonna drink to him for the time he saved my hide, and then I'm gonna bury the poor bastard. Who's gonna join me?"

Margarita nodded in reluctant confirmation, but Julia said, "I'll drink to the valiant fight he put up, but to nothing else."

"Fair enough," Sam grunted.

It was a silent toast and a quick one, then Sam left to scratch a hole at the end of the meadow to lay their companion to rest.

It took the three of them to move the body, wrapped only in a blanket, into the grave. Julia suggested a few words be said over the dead man. Sam obliged, surprising Margarita, then further amazed her by adding a few more about Bert. Both she and Sam waited respectfully while Julia cast a handful of dirt into the grave before Sam started shoveling.

While he buried Bill, the women sat before Margarita's cabin. His morbid task finished, he came over to say, "Guess I'll ride out for a while. Be back in a few days." He left them to gather his bedroll and saddlebags. In fifteen minutes he was ready.

Before he left he called Margarita aside. "Julia better be here when I get back. I gotta think over what to do about her. Have her write a letter and say she'll be away longer. It'll keep people from wonderin'. I'll mail the letter from Loma Parda."

"You'd better not," Margarita advised. "It'll arouse suspicion. A woman like Julia would never go to Parda. The place is another Sodom."

"Then I'll mail it from Sourdough."

Margarita surmised it would be better than Loma Parda, but only by a hair. "We can't keep her here forever. You'd be smarter to let her go. I don't think she'll talk about us."

"You willin' to take that chance? I'm not." He added, "I'll rustle us up a job while I'm gone."

The very thought of another holdup filled Margarita with dread. She tried to put him off. "Let's lay low for a while, Sam."

"We need the money. I'm gonna look for another stage job. No more banks. You can't get out of the damn places fast enough."

A short time later, as Julia sat at the table composing the note, she asked, "What would you do if I ran away from you while Sam's gone?"

Alarmed, Margarita looked keenly at her. Julia leave her? After all the times she had kept Sam off her back during their first days together? Defended her? Was even now trying to come up with an avenue of escape for her? "Why would you do that? I've done a lot for you — helped you."

Julia laughed without humor. "You're joking, of course."

"It's true."

"Yes, it is true. But I *am* a captive, remember? Not a visitor. You didn't have to help me."

It baffled Margarita to discover that she didn't want Julia to leave. She spoke quickly to cover this unexpected and alien sentiment. "I'd stop you. I'd have no choice. And it would probably save your life if I did. So don't try to go alone. Don't put me in that position."

Margarita paused. "It's strange," she said. She was unable to meet Julia's eyes. "I almost wish you would willingly stay, and Sam would go. Permanently. It wouldn't be so bad."

"You'd want me to live the life of a desperado? You can't be serious, Margarita."

"No, not as a desperado. I don't know what we'd do."

"Starve, that's what we'd do. You have some mighty strange ideas, the strangest being that you were once contented being a thief."

Margarita flinched at Julia's choice of words. But, yes, she had admitted she'd been satisfied with her sinister life. They had talked last night for a time in her cabin while Sam briefly spelled them both, the hypnotic sound of a heavy rain beating steadily against the roof, driving them beneath thick wool blankets, Margarita burrowing deeply in her cot with Julia in Bert's — his hauled in after they had returned from that first night's swim in the pool. Julia had not commented at the time on Margarita's revelation. From her pointed words now, it was apparent how she felt.

The letter completed, they walked over to Sam who paced restlessly before his cabin. Satisfied with the note's contents, he stuffed it into a breast pocket saying, "Remember, Margarita, she better be here when I get back."

"We're still a gang, Sam," Margarita reminded him. "I could've run out on you the day of the robbery."

"You got too much honor, Margarita. It's gonna cost you someday." He spurred his horse and rode for the trailhead.

The women headed out toward the open pasture, walking toward the horses, the herd badly depleted now because of the bank job. Margarita walked up to a big bay and rubbed his soft nose, breathing in his heavy horse smell and the odor of crushed grass still clinging to his hide where he had just rolled. He nickered and nudged her chest, pushing her back a step or two with his strong head. Scratching the big stallion behind the ears, she said, "How wonderful it would be to work with horses again. This one is such a beautiful animal. I've lost so many . . ."

"Why don't you do it?" Julia asked. "If you want to, why don't you raise them?"

"As soon as I have enough money, I will." Margarita wandered over to a sleek roan and stroked his broad muscular chest. "My husband and I used to raise crops and horses. We sold both to the army. It was a profitable business — a good life."

"Find a partner and do it again. It's honest work. Begin with these horses. Did you steal them?"

"Not all of them."

"Then start here. Get rid of your stolen goods. Give back the money."

"Never," Margarita stated quickly. "But the rest of your idea isn't a bad one. Go tell Sam to leave forever."

Julia smiled at Margarita's hopeless joke. She began picking wild flowers. "I think we should have flowers on the table every day from now on. I love color. Your place is too drab."

"By all means," Margarita agreed. "I hadn't ever thought of it myself. I used to pick flowers," she said a bit sadly, "when I was married."

"Tell me about him, Margarita. You've said so little."

"Seth was an Americano. We lived down in Lincoln County. He was killed . . . by self-appointed vigilantes." She looked southward and watched a vulture soaring majestically in the sky. "Seth died because he was married to a Mexican." She paused before continuing. "I no longer even use my married name." Margarita gazed at the open sky, then looked away toward the setting sun, shielding her eyes with a shaking hand.

"We're not all like that, you know," Julia said softly. "You mustn't hate us all. I would never knowingly hurt you."

Julia's sentiments comforted Margarita, her kind words enveloping her injured soul; they were almost the very words that Margarita had said to herself so many weeks ago as she had ridden down through the darkened canyon on her way to scout the Colter bank, thinking then of women as being the only ones who would never knowingly hurt one another.

101

On a sudden impulse Margarita said, "You could be my partner." Women were certainly strong and enduring enough for range work. Many times Margarita had ridden at her husband's side, rounding up and driving stock north to Fort Union, or had helped harvest their crops when they were desperately short of workers because everyone else was harvesting their own fields at the same time.

"With my hands?" Julia countered, reminding Margarita poignantly of her remark about how little hard work they had seen. She looked down at them, palms upward. "Although I declare, they aren't so soft anymore."

"You're learning what real work is. And you're very easy to get along with." Shyly Margarita uttered, "I . . . I like you very much. We would get along well together, I think."

After a lengthy delay, Julia replied, "I already know what real work is, Margarita. My kind of work. It would never fit in with what you would do . . . as a bandit or with horses. And I don't know if we would get along at all."

"Why not? It could work. You're a saleslady in a drugstore who knows medicine. You could doctor me, or the animals if they needed it."

"I do other things with my time."

"What kinds of things?"

Julia seemed reluctant to answer, and Margarita looked at her. Julia's face was flushed a burning red. Margarita said, "Are you all right?"

"No. Yes, I'm all right. For me, I'm all right. For you . . . for your offer, no."

Margarita cocked her head to one side. "What kinds of things do you do, Julia?" she asked again. Suspicion had already begun to creep into her mind.

"I . . . paint."

"Paint?"

Julia nodded.

"Pictures? Like those on the walls of your home?"

Again, the affirmative nod.

"Did you paint the bank wall?"

"Yes."

Margarita tightened her lips and studied the ground. She walked a short distance away and then turned to face Julia. Coldly she said, "Well then, we're even aren't we? You got us, and we got you."

Julia impatiently cast aside the flower she had been holding. "Oh, for God's sake, Margarita. I didn't get anybody."

"You got Bert and Bill."

"I did not. They got themselves and you know it. You'd do yourself a big favor if you'd quit blaming everyone else for your troubles."

"Everyone else is responsible. Even you."

"No, Margarita, I'm not. A few men are responsible for killing your husband and destroying your life, not every Anglo whoever walked the face of the earth. Whatever miseries you live with now, you've brought upon yourself."

Margarita turned from her. In the tall grass she slumped to the ground and held her head in her hands. The world seemed as black as the depths of hell.

Julia came over and sat by her side. "Listen to me." She reached out and brushed away the long hair that had fallen across Margarita's face. "I know it would go hard with you if I were to escape. An impossible task anyway. I don't know the way out of here. So, let's just try to enjoy what we have while Sam is gone."

"You painted the picture."

"All *right*, Margarita. I painted the picture! You want to start listing transgressions? Well, I can name more than a few you've dealt me. You personally abducted me from the store. You alone, Margarita. No one else helped. You also threatened someone I love. You held me captive in my own home. You stole food from me. You stole my horse. You —"

Margarita put up a silencing hand. She hadn't put things in that light. She felt her ears and cheeks burn with shame. It was some time before she could bring herself to say, "God, I'm awful, aren't I?"

Julia's next words made her feel no better. "Sometimes, yes, you are. You're terrible. Now you can make my life miserable by blaming me for having painted that damn picture, which anyone on earth might have painted, or you can let me enjoy the meadow. If I ever get out of here, I'll paint a portrait of this beautiful place. I would like to remember some good things about it. Help me do that, Margarita." Julia leaned toward her. "Can we do that?"

Give in, Margarita, she said to herself. You keep pushing her away. Give in.

She nodded wordlessly, and as they stood, Julia pulled Margarita to her and held her closely. Suspiciously, Margarita said, "You're acting this way just to make things better for yourself."

"That's true," Julia admitted. She let go of Margarita, a flush on her face. "I hope I didn't make a pest of myself."

"No . . . no you didn't."

Julia hadn't been a pest at all.

They wandered the meadow, idly picking blossoms that struck their fancy until darkness closed in. At the cabin Margarita lit several lanterns while Julia found an empty tin to hold their flowers and arranged a colorful and aromatic bouquet. "There," Julia said, "isn't that much better? Your house looks a little more like a home now and less like a desperado's hovel."

Margarita smiled and felt contented for the first time in days. "What else would you suggest we do?"

"How about curtains for the windows?"

"I don't have anything for material."

"Use your dress."

"I can't. I need it for scouting towns."

"So I've learned. Very clever."

"I thought so." Margarita spoke with some pride. "We never once got caught. Until the bank holdup, that is." Quickly she added, "But let's talk about something else." Anything would be better than mulling over the trap the gang had walked into, and what would happen now. "Tell me about yourself, Julia. How did you learn to paint?"

"Trial and error. My mother showed me some things. She used charcoal from the fireplace to draw pictures on flat stones that I would bring to her. She was very good. One Christmas my parents bought me paints from a catalogue, and some brushes. All I wanted to do after that was paint. I wasn't too interested in housework or cooking, or even in dancing, if I could paint pictures."

"Your own house is very beautiful."

"My heavy hand. It didn't look much like that before Ma and Pa died. They would have disapproved."

"Were you born in Colter?"

Julia nodded.

105

"But you never married."

"No. It doesn't seem to be the thing for me to do."

"You can't live alone."

"I probably will, though."

"Why? You're lovely. Men should be flocking to your door."

"Oh, they did at one time," Julia said, and laughed musically. "But I put them off. Most have learned. Anyway, I don't want to marry."

"I suppose you wouldn't be able to paint then."

"No, and I wouldn't be my own person any longer."

"But to live alone . . ."

"Well, who knows?" Julia answered. "My life isn't over. Anything could happen. Look what's happened so far." Playfully she reached for a towel and tossed it to Margarita. "Why don't we take a swim? It's warm enough."

They lit a lantern to guide them along the path, and in half an hour were splashing around in the darkness.

Chapter Nine

While Sam was gone the women slept late, swam frequently, and talked for hours. "How is it," Margarita asked one day, "that you recognized me the day that I . . . came to get you for Bill?"

Julia answered, "I actually thought I knew who you were a couple of weeks before that. I noticed the scar in you eyebrow the day you hit my stage. I told the sheriff about it, but since I'm a woman he thought I was likely too frightened to remember details properly. Everyone else remembered you as a half-foot taller than you are, with long greasy hair. No scar. And then that day you came in for perfume," Julia went on, "I saw the same scar. I got to thinking that Belle Starr was an outlaw, and I decided: why not? Why couldn't there be two women working outside the law?"

"When did you know for certain?"

"The day you asked me over to the window to look at the silver mirror. I could see the fear and anger in your eyes — and of course, the scar again. You were rubbing it that day — just as you're fussing with it right now."

Margarita removed her hand and smiled.

Julia asked, "What's Sam's story? Why is he an outlaw?"

"He's just loco," Margarita answered. "I don't know what drives him."

"For the first couple of days he seemed dreadfully dangerous. I had no idea that outlaws cared a hoot for one another. Your loyalties surprise me."

"Oh, Sam's all right," Margarita acknowledged. "He was frightened by Bert's death and Bill's being shot. I think he's not used to losing. It scared him. Scared me, too. Up until the bank failure I think we all thought we could go on forever, taking what we wanted, doing what we wanted."

"You're shaking." Julia took Margarita's hand in her own.

"Let's go," Margarita said, and rose to her feet. She did not want to think about how frightened she was.

Julia rose with her but when Margarita began to move away, Julia pulled her gently to her. "You'll be fine, Margarita," she whispered. Julia held her firmly in her arms, as a man might, leaving Margarita breathless and confused.

Should she pull away? Margarita wondered. Would she appear rude? Unkind? Did she care if she appeared unkind? Did an Anglo have the right to make her feel this way? To hell with it, she thought, and yielded to Julia's embrace.

They stood together for a long time before breaking apart. They embraced a second time later that day for no reason apparent to Margarita. Julia held her almost possessively, it seemed to Margarita, but again she allowed it.

As the days went by, there were more hugs, no longer just from Julia. Margarita had begun to reach for Julia. At first both sought excuses. Now none were needed. It was just a pleasant thing to do and it became a part of their day.

It wasn't quite a week later when it seemed natural that they would hold each other throughout the night, cramped and uncomfortable in Margarita's narrow cot, but willing to endure the discomfort in exchange for the closeness they now shared. They spent the next night together and the next. The following morning Margarita had to move to the other cot. She needed rest, something that hadn't occurred while they had spent the past three nights together; not while she listened hour after hour to the pounding of Julia's heart loud and clear as she lay her head against her chest, and heard her own pounding just as strongly in her own ears.

They woke late in the afternoon and stayed near the cabin until dark, waiting for the hot sun to give way to a cooler evening, planning on going for a swim.

They had bathed daily, and often after dark since that first time, Julia paddling along the shore, not yet endeavoring to move too far away from the safety of the ledge. She was insistent upon going to the pool whenever possible. A couple of days it had rained continuously, and she had expressed disappointment each time.

They took a lantern to light their way along the rocky path and in twenty minutes were splashing around in the darkness.

Margarita floated freely on her back. "I could do this all night."

Safely on the ledge of the waist-deep water, Julia walked over to Margarita and put a hand on her shoulder.

Margarita smiled in the darkness. "You're a good woman, Julia."

Without speaking, Julia easily righted Margarita from her floating position.

Slightly startled, Margarita asked, "What are you doing?"

"Margarita." She heard her name spoken in a whisper. Julia looked down on her and placed a hand on each shoulder.

A sudden and warm sensation flooded Margarita; the same sensation she had experienced that time she had gone swimming after the last stagecoach holdup while imagining kissing this Anglo.

"Margarita," Julia whispered again. Her hands moved slowly down Margarita's arms.

Margarita could feel her blood throbbing in her temples. She could barely make out Julia's features. She wished she could see clearly into Julia's eyes — to read what was there.

She remained very still, suddenly afraid that if she moved, this beautiful woman would remove her hands — and she did not want that to happen. She did not want to lose this wonderful, strange closeness.

Yielding, she allowed Julia to pull her close.

110

As their bodies came together, Margarita savored the feel of Julia's cool skin against her own, the rigid nipples pushed high against her breasts. The sensation was electrical.

"Little Yellowthroat," Julia whispered tenderly.

Over the sound of the stream emptying into the pool from above, she heard Julia's breathing, fast and labored — like her own. In another second she would want to kiss this woman. Could she do such a thing? Kiss a woman? Impossible! And then she felt Julia's lips on her own. It was not impossible at all — and the feeling was explosive.

Julia pulled Margarita more firmly against her, kissing her as aggressively as any man had ever done. Yet this was entirely different from kisses Margarita had known before. Soft lips lingered on her own, warming her with pleasure, sending piercing needles of desire throughout her body.

Something new was happening to her. She had never placed value on such intimacy as this. There had been no reason to. She had had no expectations.

Until now.

Then Julia released her.

"I . . . I'm sorry," Julia stammered. "I just don't know what got into me."

Confused and bewildered, Margarita replied, "It's all right. It's nothing."

It was everything.

She swam toward the deeper area, diving to the coldest part of the pool to cool her burning body.

Almost instantly, the air between them became silent and strained. It was as if together they had chosen to close a door between themselves by the very act of Julia's kiss. Margarita returned to the pool's edge and climbed out.

Quietly they both dressed and soon were back at the cabin asleep, each in her own cot.

The tension between them continued into the following day and the next. No longer did they hold one another, and each was very careful not to touch the other. Swimming together had ceased.

Throughout the days that followed it became difficult for them to find things to discuss, even little things. They began to snap at each other, more and more frequently until one evening they found themselves shouting over who would go after a bucket of water.

"I fetched the water the last three times!"

"I don't give a damn. Fetch it again. I'm cooking."

"Go to hell!"

"You go to hell! Today! Right now!"

Julia returned with the bucket setting it down with a heavy thud. Half of its water slopped onto the ground. "Would you look at us, Margarita? Just listen to us. Two old hens going at it like we were mortal enemies. We aren't enemies, are we?"

"No, we aren't enemies," Margarita answered coolly, patting a tortilla shell between her palms. She paused to say thoughtfully, "But I don't know what we are."

"Friends — in spite of . . . things."

"Yes, we're still friends."

Margarita warmed slightly to Julia's more cordial tone, the first she had heard her use in days.

"Aren't we good enough friends to hold one another every now and then?" Julia asked. "And should a little kiss have frightened the very devil out of us?"

It had frightened the devil out of Margarita. And she didn't remember it being a little kiss at all. Maybe only Julia had thought so.

"It shouldn't," Margarita answered tentatively. She set the tortilla in a pan and turned to Julia as she brushed her hands against the sides of her pants.

They studied each other across the log that separated them. The head of the day had left the air motionless, the clouds unmoving, the horses standing stock still with drooping heads. The only thing stirring was the rapid beating of Margarita's heart and the racing of her blood.

It wasn't clear to Margarita who moved first but the log was no longer a barrier. Once again she was in Julia's arms.

"Why did we fight, Julia?" Margarita asked, fiercely holding Julia against her. She felt the past days' tension drain from her body.

"I don't know. We're afraid, I guess."

"Of what?"

"New things. New ideas. Let's not talk about it. Just let it be enough that we aren't fighting anymore."

They laughed a lot after that, and if they came in physical contact with each other, it was lightly. But Margarita deliberately created situations. And she thought that Julia did too.

Once again they enjoyed the pool together. Day or night. And it was all right to touch one another, to embrace if it pleased them. There was nothing to be afraid of. They were friends. Margarita loved having a good friend. Not since her childhood years had she had a good friend.

Time became a pleasant blur as days and nights turned into soft memories of walking the meadow with Julia, hand in hand, or with their arms around each other's waists, binding themselves to each other, and of nights sleeping together with tender gentleness and unexplained longings.

They sat together before the cabin one evening drinking terrible coffee. "We need supplies," Margarita said. "I can't boil these grains again. I might just as well be boiling sand. Sam will be back soon. He'll bring some fresh coffee."

"Maybe I can go home," Julia offered hopefully.

"I'll try to make him understand." Margarita reached out and squeezed her arm. "Let's go to the pool. It's hot."

They swam until the moon created rippling silver rings on the warm water's surface and the air became cold and crisp. Julia floated on her back near the edge. Margarita swam over to her side and began to dunk her.

"Don't!" was all Julia managed to shout before she was submerged.

Laughing loudly, Margarita pulled her to her feet. Julia gasped and sputtered, "Damn you, Margarita. You know I hate it when you do that." She clawed strands of dripping blonde hair away from her face. Suddenly she grabbed Margarita in a bear-like hug. "You're going to be sorry this time."

There was a playful struggle between them as Julia tried hopelessly to force Margarita beneath the surface. "You're getting under," she insisted. They wrestled and tumbled in the water, neither gaining, and finally the struggle was over. Neither had won. All they had managed to do was thrash about. Margarita rested against Julia, not yet letting go, still not trusting that she wouldn't be dunked.

Julia laughed and hugged Margarita to her. "That was fun. I won."

"You did not!"

"I did too."

"You never —"

"You talk too much."

"I don't. . . ."

"Yes . . . you do."

Margarita did stop talking then, growing more and more still as Julia gazed down upon her. Frowning slightly, Margarita studied her friend. Julia wanted to kiss her again. Even in the dim light, she could read it in her eyes, feel it in her chest as it rose and fell against her own.

"Do you want to return to the cabin?" Julia asked in a low tone.

If she stepped back, Margarita knew that Julia would willingly release her. If she stepped back, she would not experience Julia's kiss, would never understand the feeling she had encountered so briefly that first time.

She breathed, "Not just yet, I don't think."

Julia's lips came down on her own. It was like before. Warm lips, terribly soft, making Margarita's head spin and her body feel as if it were not her own.

Inexplicably, Margarita had to fight putting her hands all over Julia's smooth body, but Julia was not so shy and began to kiss Margarita on her cheeks and eyes before kissing and nibbling on her neck. "My strong, strong lady."

"Julia," Margarita whispered. Her thoughts became less coherent as Julia's hands became more and more familiar. Suddenly as lost as a child, she allowed Julia to take over completely.

Julia caressed Margarita, delicately stroking her nipples, hardened not from cold water, but from Julia's fiery touch. New sensations unlike anything Margarita had ever known invaded her. It was nearly impossible to remain standing as the water gently lapped around them, while the noise of the stream kept up its musical song.

Julia, a supporting arm around her waist, must have interpreted her mind. Margarita wanted to . . . to *do* something. Unconsciously she thrust herself upward toward Julia.

Julia put a hand between Margarita's legs. An arm caught Margarita as her knees buckled, and held her steady, while strong fingers brazenly explored.

She was unable to speak, was barely able to do anything except breathe as Julia moved her fingers up and down in a slow and maddening pace, encompassing Margarita, searing her with the heat of passion.

Enflamed, Margarita moaned as a new rush of sensation grew, surpassing the last one, and the last, with each passing second until, for the first time in her life, she experienced an exploding climax that left her gasping and pulsating rhythmically inside, squeezing against Julia's fingers, with only Julia's strength holding her upright.

She could not lift her head from Julia's shoulder, could not even speak. There was a new captive at the meadow tonight.

She rested for an eternity against this unique lover, listening to impossible words spoken, wondering how Julia was so easily able to say them.

"I love you, Margarita."

"Love me? Is that possible?"

"Why not?"

"I'm a woman. How can you love me like that?"

Julia softly laughed and hugged Margarita, brushing her long hair from her shoulders. "I don't know. But it doesn't feel wrong, so I must assume it is right. It is very right for me."

"Have there been others?" Margarita asked in instant jealousy.

"No," came the slow reply. "But I've thought about women from time to time — and wondered about . . . things. . . ."

Able to stand on her own again, Margarita said reflectively, "I still don't understand."

"Don't try to, darling. Don't even waste your time. Just love me and see," Julia murmured, and guided Margarita's hand to a waiting breast.

Filled with renewed desire, Margarita freely explored Julia with wonderment, intoxicated with the softness of Julia as a woman. Tentatively she bent her head to take a nipple between her lips. Julia gasped and buried her hands in Margarita's long wet hair.

Hesitating only for a moment, Margarita slid a hand across the slight roundness of Julia's belly, then ran both hands high across her buttocks, to her hips, and finally to the inside of her thighs, where flesh and hair met.

Holding her breath, Margarita sunk beneath the water, while Julia kept her hands firmly on her shoulders. The pool was pitch black beneath its surface, as if Margarita had entered a brand new world. She buried her face against Julia, wanting to run her tongue up and down her. The urge was strong in her to do it.

She rose and led Julia to the more shallow area of the ledge. Margarita knelt again before her. She separated Julia's lips, touching a tiny mound of flesh hidden therein and experimentally thrust her tongue forward. A surge of heat raced through her, forcing her to rise, gasping as if she had been submerged beneath the water for hours.

Julia was moaning softly, her fingers still entangled in Margarita's hair.

They kissed hard and fervently. Margarita whispered, "You are more beautiful than the mountains. More beautiful than the rising sun."

117

She moved a hand down toward that area on Julia that burned like a hot branding iron within Margarita herself, and she began to explore this new kind of lover the way she had been explored. So many hidden valleys and mountains in a woman. So many secretive places. So much to give.

Margarita sucked hungrily on Julia's breasts, cool and inviting in the night. She held wide the soft lips and stroked willing flesh, strong fingers sliding over every inch of her. Julia's coarse hair felt good against Margarita's wrist and palm.

From Julia's frenzied breathing and hip thrusts, Margarita realized that she was about to do what she herself had done; go where she had gone — where Julia had taken her. She held Julia tightly around the waist, listening to her ragged breathing. Margarita's fingers within her, Julia thrust her hips in steady, pulsating motion. Margarita was heady with exotic feeling. Her head spun wildly with the incredible beauty of the moment.

Julia crushed Margarita against her and gasped, "I love you, I love you, I love you."

Margarita marveled at Julia's words. Never had she heard them spoken with such ferocity; such deep conviction.

Time passed slowly before they could breathe normally. Then together they moved to sit on a rock near the pool's edge. Still shy, they tittered as they put their arms around one another.

Margarita snuggled against Julia, savoring the closeness. Within Julia's caring encircling arms, she sighed contentedly. Life was full of wonder, of unusual twists and turns. Life was not reliable, nor even close to predictable. Who could possibly foresee, even with great wisdom, how things might turn out from day to day, even moment to moment?

"How very angry I was with you the day you came for me," Julia said. She drew Margarita even closer. "I'm not angry anymore."

Margarita knew Julia smiled. She felt her shiver. They had been out in the night air too long. "We'd better go."

They dressed, pausing frequently to kiss and to touch. As they began their descent, Margarita's head was filled with thoughts of the night ahead, those thoughts already stirring her blood.

A quick glance toward Sam's cabin with its dully lit windows told Margarita that he had returned. Entering her own dwelling, she gave him no more thought as she and Julia turned to each other in the darkness and began to help one another undress.

Chapter Ten

By mid-afternoon the following day, a single white curtain trimmed with a three-inch strip of lace hung from the window of the cabin. The material was cut not from Margarita's dress, but from her pettiskirt. With skillful fingers, Julia had sewn the little curtain while Margarita had found a willow slim enough to act as a rod. Making the curtain was only a way to fill in the time until Sam arose. The domestic activity was something more positive to do than sit and wonder and worry about what the immediate future held for Julia now that he was back.

Toward evening Sam strolled in. He inspected the cabin. "Fetchin'. Very fetchin'," he said and then walked back outside.

Margarita followed him. "How was your trip?"

"We got problems," he replied. He looked toward the cabin, making sure Julia was out of earshot. "We can't operate with just the two of us. There's extra guards on all the stages now. Wells Fargo's pissed as all hell. They ain't lettin' up for a while. Months probably." He rolled a smoke, lit it, and inhaled deeply. "I don't know what we should do."

"Who told you this?"

"Jim Nelson. I saw him in Loma Parda. Saw the stage and its guards, too. It's loaded for coyote."

"More likely, outlaws."

"Yeah." Sam crushed the half-smoked cigarette beneath his boot and tucked his hands in his back pockets. "We could get another gang together. We'd need a lot more men."

"Not much point in it is there? We never made big money with four of us. It would be even less with more men."

"What do you want to do?"

"I don't know, Sam. I wanted to buy a piece of land. We've been robbing stages for two years and I'm only about half way toward having enough money. But I'll tell you something honestly. I didn't like watching Bill go like that. It scared the hell out of me."

"Probably scared him, too," Sam answered. "Right up until he died . . . if he knew he was dyin'." He paused and then said, "Might go see my wife. Been a long time."

She wondered if Sam was dropping a broad hint that they disband. She wanted to bad enough. Still, the very idea gave her a crushing sense of defeat. She knew of no other way to earn the large amount of money that she needed. And how was she to continue taking care of her family?

"We still gotta deal with Julia, too," he added. "I'm glad to see you're both here."

Even though the words were expected, they came as a titanic blow. Yes, a rational decision did need to be made concerning their captive; some solution arrived at.

He left her standing there with her fearfully imaginative thoughts and walked toward his dwelling. Margarita barely noticed.

Filled with foreboding, she returned to her cabin and took Julia in her arms, burying her face in the graceful curve of her neck. She inhaled a lingering, musky odor still clinging to both of them. They hadn't slept for more than an hour last night, had driven one another wild until dawn. Margarita drew Julia's face to her own, kissing her long and hard.

When their lips parted, Julia said, "I want to go home, Margarita. I'm going to see Sam and tell him."

"Let's just sit for a minute first, Julia. Sam's too tired to think, and I'm too scared." She took a seat on the nearest cot.

Joining her, Julia said strongly, "I want to go home — now. He can let me go. I've done everything I'm supposed to do to . . . to behave properly, if I need to put it in such simple terms. You can guarantee I won't say anything, and so can I."

"I can't do it, Julia."

"Can't? Wasn't last night the start of something for us? Keep that before you. I want to live with you. I've already told you that I love you."

The words sounded almost silly to Margarita. "How can you possibly, Julia? I'm a woman. And a bandit, at that." Yes, what of that part of her life? Unexpectedly Margarita began to weep. She had done so many wrong things. But damn it, she had needed to.

Julia whispered, swaying the smaller woman back and forth while she held her tightly in her arms, "Perhaps it's your untamed strength that drew me to you."

"There are other strong women."

"None like Yellowthroat."

"A damn bird."

"A damn fool."

She *was* a damn fool. For a lot of reasons. One was caring too much for Julia Blake.

Margarita managed to talk Julia out of going to Sam before the following day. Then they waited until they saw him moving around later that afternoon.

"We need to talk, Sam," Julia announced as she stepped inside the door.

He waved them to the table and joined them.

"I want to go home," she told him outright. Her eyes did not waver from his.

"Well, that says it plain enough, don't it?" Carelessly he scratched the back of his head, then leaned forward on the table.

"Let her go, Sam," Margarita said.

He pursed his lips thoughtfully, then turned full attention to his captive. "I could just shoot you."

Margarita felt her skin prickle, but Julia remained calm. "You could. Are you going to?"

Sam half-smiled, saying, "I don't know."

"I don't think —" Margarita began.

"Be still, Margarita," Julia ordered. "This is between Sam and me." Her voice shook as she spoke. She was scared after all.

"No, it ain't, Julia," Sam corrected her. "It's between Margarita and me. Now you just go on out of here so's I can talk to her."

Julia rose stiffly and left, holding her head high.

Sam spoke plainly. "I'm for quittin' outlawin', for a while at least. I'm goin' down to Mexico so it won't matter if we let Julia go. If Julia squeals, it won't be no skin off my nose, just yours if you stay in New Mexico."

Margarita felt light-headed with relief. Everything was going to be all right after all. She said, "You're making it awfully easy, Sam. Why?"

"What the hell am I gonna do, keep a prisoner at the meadow for the rest of my life? I got more important things to do. You know she'd give us nothin' but trouble sooner or later. An' hell, Margarita, I just can't up and shoot a woman." His brow creased into a thoughtful scowl. "She done all right for us, too."

Sam had always liked that quality in a person. The more trouble they were willing to put up with, the more he respected them. Julia had done her share.

"So I say, break up and go our separate ways. We done all we could. Been damn lucky, too."

Margarita nodded in silent agreement. There was no other choice. She couldn't outlaw alone and she hadn't the heart to start over. At least Julia was free to leave. That was the most important consideration right now. She would worry about herself later.

"When will you go?" she asked.

"Tonight, I guess. How about you?"

"Tomorrow."

"There's just one little thing, Margarita." He scratched his chin thoughtfully. "I'm taking your cache and the extra horses with me."

"Sam. . . ."

"Go get the money."

It took only a second for Margarita to decide that to argue was to tread on deadly ground. That look was in his eye, the one that had earned him a place on the wanted posters. Oh, he wouldn't kill her. But he wouldn't be nice either. Sam could get real ugly.

She rose to go after her cache.

Chapter Eleven

As soon as Margarita had turned over her money, she and Julia packed what they would need for five days on the trail and saddled two horses. She had planned to leave tomorrow. But she could not bring herself to stay because of Sam's surprising greed. She never thought that he would rob her. They were partners. She had learned too late that when it came to money and thieves, there were no partners.

As she and Julia left the meadow, only by using iron will was Margarita able to keep her eyes straight ahead.

She fought taking a last look at the horses she loved. Right now they would be standing statuesque, deeply silhouetted against the rose-colored sky and the beautiful Sangre de Cristo Mountains that scratched the pink clouds with their lofty peaks. But the animals were now in her past; animals she loved, and had lost. She was forever becoming attached to them, only to lose one or two every few months. This time it was the entire herd. She *must* not think about it.

The women entered the canyon, the sounds of the horses' hooves mingling with the dripping walls and the creaking of leather. Within the sanctuary, Julia's voice sounded loud and out of place as she followed Margarita down the ever increasing decline of the canyon: "I'm sorry about what happened, Margarita, but I'm glad, too. It was blood money."

"I never shot anyone."

"It doesn't matter. Your friends did."

"I gave most of it to my mother."

"Does she know where it came from?"

"No."

"Don't worry, Margarita. We'll think of something soon."

That was a certainty. Margarita hadn't at all given up the idea of land and a home of her own. Not by a long shot. She would have it one day. One way or another. Being a bandito had been a failure. She was poorer now than when she had first gone to the men in Loma Parda. Now, she hadn't a peso in her pocket, and only a few dollars in the Colter Bank.

"Damn it!" Margarita shouted uselessly into the blackness of the canyon. Her voice echoed loudly off the rock walls. For all her efforts she had gained nothing. The thought hammered at her all the way down the trail.

Julia, her horse clip-clopping behind Margarita's own, said nothing.

Wanting to reach Colter as soon as possible, the women did not sleep for two nights other than dozing uncomfortably in the saddle. Exhausted and stiff, riding on tired horses, they plodded on, moving steadily northeast further and further from the meadow, eating hardtack in the saddle and grabbing sips of low-land brackish water from near-dry stream beds.

Cold nights made them shiver and the day's hot sun sapped the life out of them, leaving them limp and leaning on their mount's necks as they rode even during the hottest part of the day, their legs aching from inactivity and straddling the horses' broad backs. Sometimes they would walk to stretch a little, but continued moving steadily toward Colter. They barely spoke to one another during their journey, Margarita still angry and Julia apparently too tired to care.

"I can hardly stay in this saddle," Julia groaned on the third evening. They had only twenty-five miles to go but it might as well have been a million to Julia, who had reached her limit. Tears she could not control filled her eyes. As close as they were to Colter, Margarita knew they must stop for the night.

She suddenly hated herself for having brought her lady into this mess. Her lady? The words startled her. She had not thought of Julia in those terms before. Sadness filled her, and she had an overwhelming need to hold Julia to her breast and bear her discomfort for her.

They stopped along a small stream. "We'll rest here tonight," she said. "We've pushed hard enough."

Julia slid from the saddle. Margarita helped her over to a downed piñnon tree lying beside the shallow rivulet and eased her into a seated position.

"I'll be so glad to be back in my own clothes," Julia moaned. "And no longer on a horse. I'll never ride one of these beasts again."

The horses wandered over to the stream and sucked thirstily, too tired to roam more than a few feet from their riders.

On her knees, Margarita moved between Julia's legs and put her arms around her. She kissed her softly. Julia pulled back from Margarita and whimpered slightly.

"What is it?" Margarita had been gentle. She had always been gentle with Julia.

"It's my legs. The saddle sores."

"Let me see."

"It's nothing. Don't bother."

"I insist." Margarita spoke firmly. Unattended saddle sores could turn into crippling injuries.

Julia pulled off a boot and worked a pant leg and long underwear partially up her leg. A large, oozing wound covered the inside of her left calf.

"My God, Julia, why didn't you say something before this?"

"I didn't want to take the time to stop. I'm still a little scared Sam might follow."

Margarita sighed. "Don't be. He's headed for Mexico. Now we must take care of you. Get undressed."

While Margarita untied the medicine bag from behind her saddle, Julia took off her clothes. "Men wear the damnedest clothing," she complained harshly. "You can't even take off your damn drawers without getting completely undressed."

Margarita laughed at Julia's anger. "You look good to me." Unbearably tired though she was, she could still easily admire Julia's firm breasts and smooth skin. She wished that they were both back at the meadow standing in the pool, their skin caressed by the cool air and warm water of the night. She wrapped a blanket around the shivering woman and turned her mind to tending Julia's leg.

Julia drew the blanket tighter to her body, leaving the underwear hobbling her ankles while Margarita rubbed salve on the wounds of her thighs and calves. She wrapped them with strips of cloth. "It isn't the best way to take care of you, but it'll have to do."

Julia stood and began to dress. "I'll survive."

"Think of all the stories you'll have to tell your grandchildren." Margarita chuckled as she helped Julia button her shirt.

Frowning, Julia replied, "I thought you understood, Margarita, that you're the one I'm spending my life with."

Embarrassed, Margarita stammered, "Oh, yes, certainly. I was only joking."

She hadn't been joking at all. She did not feel comfortable with Julia's apparent firm decision. In fact, she felt trapped by it. She had other things in life planned for herself — her own future. And in the long run, Julia was not a part of that. For now, what they shared was fine. It was wonderful. But she couldn't get into a discussion about it now. They were both too tired.

She left Julia near the log and walked over to unsaddle the horses. When she returned, Julia was fast asleep. Margarita looked at her for a long time, studying her, wondering why she didn't feel as strongly about their relationship as Julia did. "I wish I could love you," Margarita quietly confessed. "But still, I care more for you than I ever have for anyone, even Seth — and that's a lot."

She eased her lover into a better position, putting her hat under her head for a pillow. Julia never stirred at the repositioning of her body, inhaling and exhaling in deep exhausted breaths.

Margarita tied the horses to the piñon tree and straddled the trunk to stand guard, then threw both legs to one side. The log felt too much like a horse. For once in her life, she was sick of riding like a man.

Julia shook Margarita's shoulder. It was almost dawn. "I feel better, Margarita. Let's go."

Margarita lifted her chin from her chest. "Oh, my neck. I think it's broken." She massaged it with one hand. "Lord, I didn't mean to fall asleep."

"No harm done. Let's go."

"You're horrid," Margarita accused affectionately, giving Julia a squeeze, and went to prepare the horses. Soon they were riding through the early morning dawn toward Colter.

Chapter Twelve

Upon entering the house, Margarita was struck by a strong unpleasant smell, probably caused by the place being shut up for so long. Wrinkling her nose she remembered the same smell, only weaker, when she had been here before. Perhaps a dead rat or some such animal had been trapped somewhere in the house and was rotting away. The odor wasn't quite right, but she could not think of anything else it might be. But she noticed that Julia had taken a long, deep, and, it seemed to Margarita, almost sensuous breath when she had first set foot through the door.

"What is that odor?" Margarita questioned.

"It's paint," Julia replied. "Upstairs. It's always this powerful whenever I've been away for a while and the house is closed up. I go up there first thing. Makes me feel at home again just to look around the room."

They dumped their belongings on the kitchen table. Margarita followed Julia through the parlor and up the narrow stairs she had climbed seemingly centuries ago. "You didn't see this room," Julia said as they reached the landing, "the last time you were here." She led the way to a door at the end of the hall and opened it, stepping aside to let Margarita enter first.

The odor was ten times as strong here as anywhere else in the house. Countless tubes of paint cluttered narrow tables placed along the walls. Stacks of canvas, some complete, others half finished, filled the space beneath the tables. Two oils sat on easels, both depicting ranch scenes. Most of the paintings were of New Mexico Territory, and Margarita wondered who in the world would want pictures of this land. She picked up an almost empty, badly mutilated tube of paint. "Where do you get all this?"

"I send to New York or Chicago for most of it," Julia replied. "Some paints I make from pulverized rocks of different colors, mixed with oil. Or I'll use certain plants and oil. Sometimes if I can't get the oil I need to make the paint, I have to use eggs. But I prefer oil. The color is richer, better. Paint made with eggs will fade in the long run."

"You're a very serious *artista*, aren't you?"

"The day you saw me on the stagecoach, I was on my way to Albuquerque. I thought I might be able to find

133

some plants or stone to use for new colors. Your taking my money forced me to return to Colter." She picked up a fistful of brushes, running the palm of her hand across the bristles.

"I'm sorry," Margarita said, and she truly was. A thought crossed her mind. "Is that why Henry asked you about bringing back new dust from your trip that day we left for the meadow?"

"That's what he meant."

Margarita stopped before a large canvas of the craggy and beautiful Sangre de Cristo Mountains, the colors sharp and clean, the oil applied with thick bold strokes. "You're very good, you know." She turned toward Julia who stood in the doorway. "I'm glad Sam never knew."

Julia agreed wholeheartedly. "I'd love to go to work right now, but I need to eat, bathe, and then sleep for three days without moving. I don't know what there is to eat, but anything is better than tortillas and beans."

After resting the three full days that Julia had demanded, they drove to Colter. It was time to let Henry know she was back. She had been gone almost a month. It would be Julia's sole income that would sustain the two of them, and she needed to resume work.

As Margarita walked with Julia into the drugstore, it was a different feeling she carried with her today. No longer a bandito, she saw things with new eyes. She didn't have the little knot of fear she had always carried with her during reconnaissance. Until this moment she hadn't even realized that it had been an integral part of her life these past two years. Julia had given her money to buy some soaps and salves while in town, and she would happily pick these items up, not as an excuse to cover

134

devious behavior, but for actual need of them. She felt giddy with exhilaration and freedom.

Maude turned at the jingling of the bell. The two women walked over to a counter where she was busily dusting. The old man was nowhere in sight.

"Hello, Maude," Julia said with a smile.

"You're back," Maude replied.

She sounded less than enthusiastic, and Margarita recalled her dislike of the caustic woman from the previous time they had met.

"Back and ready to work," Julia said.

Leaving Julia to her business, Margarita walked away to study the perfumes displayed on a nearby counter. She had never gotten as good a look at them as she had wanted to before. That times seemed a century ago.

"I'm afraid not, Julia Blake. You won't be needed here any longer." Maude's tone was blunt.

Not needed? Margarita turned to listen.

"Don't be silly, Maude. I've been here for years. Of course I'm needed."

"No longer, Julia. Henry has died."

"Died? When?" Tears sprang to her eyes. Margarita knew that she had loved the old man.

"He breathed his last three weeks ago. Just up and went to glory in his sleep. No warning whatsoever."

"I can see his death affected you deeply," Julia said sarcastically, "and you his grandniece."

"Oh, you'll be affected, too. As you know, I was his oldest living relative." Maude paused and a little smile creased her slit of a mouth. "He left the entire store to me. That's what he thought of you. And I'll be operating the business alone. He should have had me working here all along, so I've only gotten what should have been rightfully mine to begin with."

"What about those who need Julia's medical help, Maude?" Margarita had walked to Julia's side, angered by Maude's coldly superior attitude.

"I'll take care of them," Maude said pridefully. "I've been reading Uncle Henry's medicine books and I've helped a couple of people already."

Her haughtiness infuriated Margarita. She could not help asking, "Did they live?"

"Of course they lived," Maude responded sharply. "Do you have any business to conduct here? I'm quite busy today."

"I can see that you are," Margarita answered, and pointedly looked around the empty store. She would shop elsewhere. Colter was big enough. "How is it," she asked, "that Julia, instead of you, worked here if you were old Uncle Henry's relative?"

"That's none of your business."

Margarita smiled carelessly and sauntered out of the store, Julia following closely behind. Margarita spat on the sidewalk in front of the door. So much for loyalty.

Within an hour, the despondent women sat at the kitchen table.

"Well, blood is thicker than water in the end, isn't it?" Julia said angrily. "There's no accounting for how men will behave. Damn old Henry, anyway. I really thought he cared about me, that he'd make sure I'd continue working there no matter who he left the place to. I used to do for him constantly."

"Why *did* you work there, instead of Maude?"

"Because she's totally incompetent, that's why." Julia fought tears of disappointment. "Henry *knew* that!"

"She thinks she's doing a fine job."

"Oh, she'll get by, I suppose. But she's always struck me as a crabby old biddy. It was hard not to let her know I felt that way. I guess I didn't. I hate to think what will happen to the store now."

"Why don't you see if she'll sell the business to you? You know more than she does. You'd have a position, security. . . ."

"That's out of the question. I'm almost without funds. I've spent nearly every dime I've ever earned on paints and canvas." Standing abruptly she said, "I can't think about this anymore. I'll be upstairs." Quickly she left the room.

Margarita understood that no more was to be said about the drugstore or Maude, now or ever.

Following her to the bedroom, Margarita said, "Let's give ourselves a half hour, Julia. We need to be together."

Julia nodded her agreement. Her depression had obviously reached the same depth as Margarita's own.

Margarita left to seal the house. She returned to find Julia undressed and lying on the bed. With outstretched arms Julia said, "Come here."

Margarita hurriedly removed her clothing, thinking how like an order Julia's words had sounded. As Margarita lay down by her side, Julia pulled her firmly against her. "You're so aggressive," Margarita said, not quite able to adjust to this side of her lover, and unsure whether she liked it or not. She remembered that Julia had been like this back at the cabin, too. She just didn't look the type to be so forward — but then what exactly did a forward woman lover look like? Or do? Margarita had no idea. She wasn't even sure if what they had together was real to begin with.

"What difference does it make if I'm aggressive or not, as long as you like what I do and I don't hurt you?" Julia pulled Margarita even tighter against her.

"I don't know," Margarita answered. "I just never thought of a woman as making bold advances in bed."

"That's nonsense, Margarita. If you want to take command in this bed, take command. If you don't want to, then don't. Do what you want to do, not what you think you're supposed to do." She kissed Margarita on the tip of her nose, each eyelid, then softly began to nibble on a dark earlobe.

Margarita made an effort to readjust her thinking. She didn't remember having this problem back at the cabin when she had been with Julia.

In the sealed room with only a single open window to let in the slightest of breezes, their bodies were slick with sweat. Julia lowered herself on top of Margarita and began to move up and down, the moisture between them eliminating friction. Her head was thrown back, her eyes closed.

Margarita pulled the hairpins from Julia's long tresses, releasing them to fall free and loose across her face and chest. She pulled Julia's face to her own, kissing her through damp heat and disarrayed strands of silken hair. She spread her legs wide to allow Julia to nestle between them, and, pushing against her, felt her lover's sensual body begin to press slowly and firmly against her.

Margarita relinquished guilt-ridden thoughts of men and concentrated only on the woman now breathing heavily into her ear. Julia easily slid a hand between their bellies as Margarita wrapped her in her arms. She felt Julia's fingers reach and explore, felt Julia move her hips and hand at the same time, finally entering Margarita and moaning as she caused searing heart to build within Margarita. Julia was going to take her to that place again — that place she had never been before with anyone except this incredible *amante.*

"Ahhh," she shouted joyously as she came in a blinding climax while Julia bent her head to suck on a swollen, dark brown nipple.

"Stop," Margarita said in a whisper.

But Julia either didn't hear or deliberately paid no heed as she continued to manipulate Margarita, sliding a finger in . . . out . . . in . . . out. . . .

Resisting her sensations, Margarita said, "Julia . . . wait. . . ."

But again, Julia didn't respond. "Stop fighting me, Margarita," she whispered. "You love me and you know it. Why do you fight me?"

And again a searing flame shot through Margarita as Julia brought her wildly to another climax and then a third, and a fourth.

At last, Julia pulled her hand away.

Margarita forgot her earlier resistance to Julia and seized her with near madness as passion continued to possess her. Effortlessly she changed positions with Julia, rolling her over and laying full length upon her, driving her hips into her.

While Julia whispered, "Harder," in a hoarse voice, Margarita pleaded with her to let her bury herself in Julia's body.

Julia pushed Margarita's head down toward her thighs. "Now," she shouted, and Margarita's tongue drove fiercely into her.

"I want you, I want you," Margarita moaned into the soft wetness of Julia's body.

She could not do without her.

Julia arched, arched again, then lay still.

Margarita got up on her hands and knees and bent to dry her face on Julia's stomach, savoring the feel of her satin skin.

"Come here," Julia said, and drew Margarita up to her side. "Put your hand here." She guided Margarita between her legs, then Julia put her own hand on Margarita. "Now, together," she said, and began to move rhythmically.

Margarita followed Julia's lead until she could no longer think. But she didn't need to think anymore. Both women were gasping and clutching at each other, whispering endearing words, holding one another tightly until the highest point of passion finally freed them; until they both fell apart and then lay still.

Julia whispered softly, "How I love you, Margarita Sanchez. I thank God you were a bandito."

For a long moment Margarita did not answer, waiting for her pounding heart to still. "A terrible life. I realize that now."

"I don't care. It brought us together."

"Yes, it did that." Margarita again felt trapped, forgetting that just moments before she had thought she could not live without Julia. Was it only the act of love itself, then, that made Julia so attractive to her? Considering all the men she had been with, it was best with Julia.

Julia smiled a brilliant smile. Margarita buried her face in the large feather pillow, the unidentifiable ache in her chest toward this woman, the wanting of her, almost more than she could endure, leaving her confused and deeply troubled.

Chapter Thirteen

For the next couple of days, the women dusted and swept and scrubbed vengefully, neither liking housework, but putting up with it all the same. On the third day Julia threw down her broom. "I'm sick of this! Let's go to town."

In twenty minutes they were ready.

Julia parked the buggy two doors down from the Low Dog Saloon. She would see Belle, a dancehall girl and a long time acquaintance, who would slip her a bottle of good red wine.

"You're friends with a saloon girl?" Margarita asked incredulously.

"And a bandit, too," Julia answered lightly, leaving Margarita standing in the wake of her own embarrassment as she disappeared behind the Low Dog.

Margarita wandered up and down the sidewalk gazing in windows, admiring hats and dresses that were now completely out of her reach. Fifteen minutes later, Julia rejoined Margarita at the buggy with a brown paper bundle tucked under her arm. After stashing the wine beneath the seat, they strolled the sidewalks and wandered in and out of stores for the better part of the morning.

People stopped Julia numerous times to discuss her dismissal from the drugstore, all of them professing to be sorry as sin to hear she wouldn't be working there any more. Would she still be helping the doctor? Could she come see their children? Tommy had been sick as a dog, but the doctor had saved him. But if she had been there, he would have gotten better faster. The litany of praise went on and on. Margarita couldn't remember all the people she herself had been introduced to.

"You're well thought of," Margarita remarked at the buggy's side as Julia was able to at last free herself from a final conversation.

They climbed onto the seat. "I have something they want."

"It must be nice."

"Oh, don't be so touchy. I've never made a half-dime out of it."

That made Margarita feel better. Then she felt worse. They were both nearly penniless except for the pittance each still had in the bank.

On the way out of town, Margarita said almost desperately, "We've got to do something, Julia. We are poor. Poor!"

"We'll work something out. I'll start thinking tomorrow. That'll be time enough. Tonight . . . there's wine." She gave Margarita a little nudge and leaned against her meaningfully, apparently her depression of yesterday gone with today's warm reception around town.

"I think we need to discuss this now." Margarita was dreadfully afraid of being destitute. She had lived that way in Carizaillo. She didn't want to go through such agony again.

"No, tomorrow is soon enough," Julia said firmly. "I'm too tired to do that kind of planning."

Margarita turned angrily in her seat. "You know what I'm tired of, Julia? I'm tired of worrying if we can grain the horses. I'm tired of worrying if I'll be able to buy flour enough to bake a tortilla shell or . . . or a loaf of bread, or something special like a pie, let alone put something in its shell. And, I'm damn *scared* of being poor again!"

Julia reined the horse to an abrupt halt. "What a notion!" Her eyes sparkled as she turned to Margarita. "What an idea, you wonderful woman!"

"Julia, damn it —"

"No, listen to me. You're not going to starve. *We're* not going to starve. We're going to make money. Lots of it. We can bake bread, pies, cookies. That's exactly what we'll do. I can decorate them up fancy. I'm an artist."

"People are already doing that."

"Not like this." Julia was animated. Her eyes flashed as her hands moved rapidly through the air. "We could sell our goods all over Colter, fresh off the back of the wagon. And we could go door to door. Personal delivery. People know me. They trust me. It would work,

Margarita. I know it would! You're brilliant, just brilliant!"

So Julia had been just as worried. An enormous weight lifted from Margarita's shoulders at the thought of a possible way out of their immediate poverty. And she felt very contrite. "I . . . I'm sorry I yelled at you, Julia."

"Oh, to hell with that. I'm glad you did." She dismissed Margarita's former ire with a flip of her hand. "Look at the marvelous idea you've given us."

Immensely relieved of their most pressing problem, they laughed and whistled and sang songs and stumbled over the words because one sang in English and the other in Spanish. And neither knew any song that the other knew.

The following morning they were in town at eight, going first to the bank. They drew out their remaining savings. With this slim amount they would begin their business.

Margarita had to fight against staring at the spot where Bert had died. She fought, too, against looking at the painting on the wall. She knew that keenly alert men stood behind those people's eyes, just waiting for some fool to do something stupid. To look up there would be *estupido*! She left with the remnants of her cache as quickly as possible.

They drove over to the emporium with a list they had carefully prepared last night tucked in Julia's purse. They had planned to the penny what to buy and together had tallied the house's staples, canned goods, and dried fruit left from last season. The fruit was scant and probably should have been eaten by now but would do in a pie with an extra pinch of sugar. Nothing must be wasted.

"Morning, Clare," Julia called out cheerily as she and Margarita entered the store.

"Morning, Julia," came a voice from behind a counter somewhere near the rear of the building. "Maude said you were back. Welcome."

Margarita inhaled the rich aroma of freshly ground coffee, of dill pickles fermenting in brine in open oak barrels. Three women to her left chatted and looked at bolts of muslin, calico, and domestic, both bleached and unbleached, both of a light and heavy weave. Skirts, shirts, and drawers were made from the lighter material and sacks for corn and other grains from the heavier cloth. Women's shawls for both summer and winter lay stacked high beside bolts of cloth and piles of blankets. Ginghams for cheap dresses and aprons, and stockings, both woolen and cotton, and ribbons were laid out next to the blankets.

Sacks of sugar, brown and white, sat behind the store's front counter, the white granulated or cubed, the cubed being preferred by campers should the sugar spill. There were bags of coffee, boxes of crackers, bars of chocolate, and other sweets that made a body's mouth water just looking at them. There were sperm whale candles, and coal oil too, less popular because of the outrageous price, and some lard and tallow for those who did not have their own hogs or cattle. A large supply of dried apples and peaches was piled alongside plums and pears. There were even canned sardines and oysters.

Julia walked over to the counter. A tiny freckled-faced woman, her flaming red hair braided around her head, rose from behind the counter. She set a large wood box down with a grunt. "Got to get these canned goods out this morning. William was supposed to do it yesterday but he got the fever and went hunting."

145

Julia smiled and handed Clare their carefully planned list. "Can you fill this?"

"Hmmm, dried peaches and apples, canned pears, lard. . . . You still have pecans from last year, Julia? It'll save you a bucket of money." Clare didn't bother to wait for an answer. She began to fill the order, stacking the items on the counter before her. "Twenty-five pounds of flour, sugar. . . . You want white sugar, don't you? Five pounds of salt. . . . Eggs. . . . Fresh eggs just this morning, Julia. Brought in by Abigail Kirby."

As Clare gathered the groceries together, Margarita looked over a dozen different kinds of sweets displayed handsomely on the counter eye level to a small child. She would love the richness of a licorice root or the tang of a mint stick; just seeing them through those glass cylinders made her mouth water and her jaws ache.

Overhead and against the walls hung pots and pans, tin plates and cups with iron knives and forks, frying pans, and Dutch ovens, washboards and tubs. Beneath these for no logical reason were shelves of spices. Margarita squinted at tins of cinnamon, nutmeg, pepper, bay leaves, dry mustard, oregano, chili powder, and red pepper.

As the wall clock chimed nine, Margarita sat down in a chair next to a cold pot belly stove. Warily she eyed four freshly baked pies protected from buzzing flies by a curved glass case and prominently displayed on a nearby counter. A second case, three-tiers high with a sliding back door, held two cakes. She could see Julia looking obliquely at the same case as she stood in front of the counter seemingly studying the label on one of the cans of pears Clare had just placed there. The baked goods looked good. So they would have competition. But that went without saying. Any woman worth her salt could cook and bake.

"That's everything, Julia," Clare said. "I'll get one of the boys to load for you. You must be hungry for sweets."

Julia smiled but did not explain.

"Now comes the serious part," Julia said as they headed for home. "We've got enough wood to keep the oven going all day long for the next few days, but after that we'll have to hire more cut and split. We'll have to pay from our profits."

"It's going to take a while to see daylight, isn't it?" Margarita asked a bit wistfully.

Julia nodded. "We'll just keep plugging. We should be able to earn enough to feed ourselves and keep ourselves in firewood this winter, and still have a little extra for your mother, but that'll probably be about it."

"I thought you said yesterday that we'd be rich."

"I lied."

"I thought so." But it was all right because Margarita felt closer to Julia today than she had yesterday . . . than she had the day before, or last week.

She believed they would be successful if they put their minds to it. Working with Julia would be better than working with Sam and Bill and Bert had ever been. Probably harder, too — but far, far safer. Again, she felt an exhilarating surge of relief that her outlawing had been left behind — and that she had never been wounded or caught or hanged.

The women rose at four the following morning to take full advantage of the night's cooler temperatures.

Over the next three days they mixed and kneaded dough for bread and cookies; and pastry for pies of pecan, peach, and apple, their shells filled until they were nearly overflowing. They whipped batter and baked. Last, they

147

made tiny, fancy cakes and cookies that could be sold individually and directly from the wagon.

Each afternoon the heat in the kitchen became almost unbearable. Sweat soaked their clothing and the scarves that held back their hair. They went barefoot and stockingless, wearing only light gingham dresses; they shed their underwear and pinned up the waists of their dresses, raising the skirts a good two feet off the floor to allow for as much comfort and air circulation as possible.

In the oppressive heat, bumping into each other as they worked steadily to meet their preset three-day deadline, they snapped at each other, held one another, kissed, made up, snapped again, and remained on schedule.

Baking continued until darkness fell, the food placed on a table they had hauled into the front room and then covered with a clean bed sheet to protect it from insects.

The women staggered upstairs each night, the entire house smelling of baked goods. They fell asleep in one another's arms as soon as their heads hit the pillow, not moving until four the following morning.

"*Gracias a Dios*, we're done," Julia said as she lay down the third night.

Margarita wanted to talk but she could feel sleep overpowering her.

"We can lay in bed until six tomorrow," Julia told her. "We'll take the wagon and both horses. It won't take us long to load."

"Margarita?" Julia let out a contented sigh. "*Buenas noches*, my brave lady."

Margarita backed the wagon up to the kitchen door, clucking to the team, pulling and tugging on the reins until the vehicle was within two feet of the building. Under a cloudless and warm morning, they loaded bags and boxes of cakes, pies, cookies, and bread, all ready to be driven to Colter.

Wearing plain cotton dresses, light pettiskirts, and sun bonnets, they ate a quick breakfast of several too-done cookies and half a loaf of bread, not even wanting to look in the direction of the oven.

Although they were both so tired that dark rings circled their eyes and their bodies lagged, they were full of hope and enthusiasm. "I'll bet we come back with an empty wagon," Julia said happily.

"And pockets full of money."

"That too," Julia agreed.

The women climbed onto the seat and Margarita clucked the team into motion. Julia opened a parasol to shade herself against the sun's strong rays. She said, "We already know that we daren't charge higher prices than our competitors. But if we undercharge, we'll have the restaurants angry with us, the emporium, the general store . . . any of those places that sell baked wares. We certainly don't want that."

"Where do those particular goods come from?" Margarita asked.

"From the wives. We won't go near those stores. We'll sell to cowboys . . . the tellers in the bank . . . the smithy."

"What about going over to the railroad station when the train comes in?"

"Good idea. We'll also see the barber . . . the doctor . . . I know he'll buy at least one cake. We'll go there first thing. We'll also go by the sheriff's office, the telegraph office. . . . We could try the back doors of the saloons."

"To hell with that," Margarita put in. "I'll walk right through the front door. They will be unable to resist the *hermosa viuda.*" She made flashing eyes at Julia.

"They'd better resist her," Julia answered possessively. "She belongs to me."

Margarita fought off a sudden oppressive feeling and thought, *I belong to no one.* But aloud she replied, "Let's go to the millinery's, too."

They went first to Doc James' office only to find him away. "He's never in," complained Julia. They were filled with unexpected disappointment at not making an immediate sale, and it sent just a little scare into them, which, they admitted to each other, was quite groundless because they had the entire day before them and, of course, almost the entire town. Still, a fast successful sale had been important to them.

"Well then, let's go to the sheriff's office," Julia suggested.

"Now?"

"Certainly," Julia pronounced confidently. "Why not now? He needs to eat, too. And he's only right next door."

"I was hoping to leave him until last. Maybe we'd have run out of goods by then."

"Oh, don't be a *cobarde,*" Julia teased. "Besides, he may even have a prisoner or two with a dollar left in their pockets after a night at the gaming tables."

Sighing with resignation, Margarita steered the wagon toward the sheriff's office. "Life is strange," she muttered to no one, and joined Julia at the door.

Sheriff Hoskins sat tipped back in a chair, his feet propped up on his desk, its worn and scarred surface heaped with piles of paper. Margarita could hardly keep from wrinkling her nose at the stinking smoke collecting in the small room, emitting from Hoskin's long, pungent cigar.

"Hey, looka them little gals," called a lone prisoner, unkempt and heavily bewhiskered, from a cot in the jail's only cell off to the right of the office. His words were slurred. Unsteadily, the man sat up and squinted through puffy eyes at Julia and Margarita. Then he staggered over to the cell door and gripped the door's bars and coughed long and hard, his lungs rattling with phlegm. With shaking hands, he began to roll a cigarette.

"Shut up, Jones," ordered the lawman sternly, dropping his feet to the floor. "You ain't even sober yet."

"I ain't blind drunk, neither," came the happy, grinning response as the prisoner continued to eye the women. "Wal, hell, if it ain't Miss Julia."

She spoke crossly to him. "Marcus Jones, you should be ashamed of yourself."

"Wha' fer?" he asked belligerently.

Julia turned back to the sheriff, ignoring Jones. Sheriff Hoskins rose. "Good to have you home, Julia. Somebody said you were back."

"Back and working," Julia declared. "Sheriff, meet Margarita Sanchez." She turned toward her lover. "She and I bake pies, cakes, cookies, and loaves of bread. All fresh, all available — right now, out in the wagon."

"I wanna pie!" the prisoner roared loudly, grabbing the bars of the cell.

"You ain't gettin' no pie," pronounced the sheriff over his shoulder.

"I got some money left," Jones announced. "What kinda pie an' how much?" He began to search through his pockets.

As Hoskins began to speak to the prisoner again, Margarita surprised herself by saying, "Oh, let him buy a pie, Sheriff. It'll help his morale, being cooped up like this." But for a long run of good luck, it could have been her behind those bars.

The sheriff eyed Jones warily. "Money up front, Marcus. How much you got?"

"I know I got a half-dollar left. Must be in my boot." He sat on his cot and began to pull off a badly worn boot.

"I'm sorry, Marcus Jones. Pies are fifty-five cents," Julia expressed firmly.

"For a damn half-dime, you wouldn't sell a pie to a condemned man?" Jones wailed pathetically. "I wanna pie, damn it."

"You ain't a condemned man, Jones," Hoskins retorted. "You'll be out by noon if you go back to sleep."

"I want a damn pie!"

The sheriff turned to Julia. "Oh, hell, let him have the pie for fifty cents."

Margarita's stomach knotted up. If Julia let the pie go for a half-dime less, there would be other cuts in prices, given as simple favors just because someone was a little short of funds . . . or Julia's friend . . . or for some other crazy reason.

"I'm sorry, Sheriff," Julia said more purposefully than before. "But we need the money as badly as he needs the pie. Business is business. It's another five cents or he gets nothing from us."

Margarita collapsed inwardly with relief, breathing once again. She had not wanted to step in and intercede on the business's behalf on their very first sale. But she would have if Julia hadn't stood her ground. And it pleased her exceedingly that Julia had used the words 'we' and 'us' without wavering, indicating strongly that they were in this together.

"I need the pie," Jones wailed. "I *neeeed* it."

"Aw right, Jones. Quit your caterwaulin' and you'll get your damn pie. I'll give you the half-dime for him, Julia, just to shut him up. Bring me a loaf of bread, and a chocolate cake if you got it."

"What kind of pie would you like, Marcus?" Julia asked. "We have pecan. . . ."

"Pecan!"

Margarita fetched the men's orders and placed them carefully on the desk. Hoskins leaned toward Jones' pie and inhaled deeply. "Hmmm, smells good."

"Get your nose offen my pie, damn yuh!" Marcus Jones snarled.

Hoskins paid Julia, and as the women left they could hear the two men growling at each other over exchanging an honest piece of pie for an honest piece of cake. "It's a wonder the sheriff doesn't shoot Señor Jones," Margarita stated as she drove toward the train station.

"That'll never happen. They're the best of friends."

"You joke with me."

Julia smiled and shook her head. "For years and years. They even ride posse together now and then — when Marcus is sober long enough to stay in the saddle, which isn't often."

The women reached the station in time to sell several dozen cookies and two pies to exiting and departing passengers who paid hurriedly, anxious to be on their way.

They returned to the doctor's office again. Thankfully James had returned, and in no time Julia had sold him a cake just as she had predicted. They stopped at the stores they had chosen, and then at ten o'clock they worked the saloons, which were beginning to get a little busy by now. Margarita walked brazenly into each one, carrying wares

153

with her and coming out empty-handed only a short time later.

Sold last, the individual fancy cookies were favorites of the children, and especially of the ladies. They had seen or heard what the women were up to and had come over to talk and admire, glad to try foods which they knew took hours to make. And they wished to secretly compare Julia and Margarita's baking with their own.

At eleven o'clock the wagon was empty.

It was time to head for home.

Chapter Fourteen

Margarita and Julia danced arm in arm around the kitchen table, whooping and singing over the small stack of money lying in its center. As soon as they had returned from town and had turned the team out, they had hurried inside, emptied their purses' contents, and gleefully counted out the day's earnings.

Babbling and giggling, they divided the grand total into several piles, setting each one in a different area of the table. First and foremost was the money to restock those items they could not keep, such as eggs and milk, or to replace what they had exhausted on their first baking spree, such as their twenty-five pounds of flour. Another pile was for firewood, another for food, and finally, a small emergency fund. They compared the totals against what they had estimated and jotted them down in a little notebook, and, yes, they had cleared ten dollars. It wasn't a fortune, but it was a start.

Their initial joy over, they relaxed at the table, sipping coffee that Julia had heated outside over a small fire, and discussed their morning's adventure, all the while fingering a bill or turning a coin over and over in their hands. "Maybe we could have a little showcase built to put on the end of the wagon," Julia said.

"When our profit pile is higher," Margarita suggested, and thumbed the small stack of dollars lying there. "There were a few times when I raked in hundreds, and it took only minutes. So I don't know why I'm so excited about this measly ten dollars."

"Maybe because you earned it honestly," Julia teased. She hid behind her cup, a half-smile playing on her lips.

Margarita's thoughts became dark, and a scowl crossed her face. "I guess it's time to start thinking smaller." Julia placed a hand over her own. She let out a mournful sigh. "Don't worry, I'll be fine." She stood and walked around Julia's chair. Leaning over her, she wrapped her arms around her and breathed in her fragrance. "You smell lovely."

"I smell like a cookie."

Margarita laughed. It was pleasing to hold Julia whenever she wanted to, to be loved by her, to be held by her at night. "You mean very much to me, Julia," she whispered, and kissed her ear through fine blond hair.

"How much do I mean to you?"

"More than you know."

"More than *you* know, you mean," Julia said. She rose and took Margarita in her arms.

"What do you mean?"

"You really don't know, do you?"

"No . . . I guess not."

"You will."

"When?"

"When you figure out who you are."

"I know who I am."

"But you don't know what you want. I know, but you don't."

"How could you know, and not me?"

"I don't know . . . but . . . I can wait until you do." Julia's breathing was steady but deep. "Shall we go upstairs?"

"*Sí.*"

Julia locked the door, and hand in hand they walked up the narrow stairs to the bedroom. Quietly and slowly, each carefully disrobed, dropping her dress over a chair while watching the other, already making love with their eyes.

They moved to the bed and lay down. Julia took Margarita in her arms and began to run her hand slowly across Margarita's belly, occasionally circling her navel with a slender finger.

Margarita let herself go, relaxing completely, not thinking of men or of Julia's more active role, the one she always took first.

Margarita felt she was learning how to love this woman. It was all right to go just a little mad with passion. It was acceptable to love Julia as strongly as she desired. Julia wanted her that way . . . liked it . . . cried for it at times.

157

Pleasant thoughts drifted in and out of her mind as her lover continued to caress her. She pulled Julia on top of her. She wanted to feel Julia's weight, her bones grinding into her flesh.

Julia accommodated Margarita not only with her hips but with her hands, exploring, seeking, moving . . . in constant motion, tantalizing and exciting, making Margarita want her more and more.

"I can love you better than anyone else," Julia uttered.

"Yes," Margarita whispered fiercely. "I want no one but you." There was no one who could love as Julia could love.

She gasped in ecstasy as Julia encircled each nipple with sensuous lips while holding her tightly with a strong arm. Julia slid a hand between their bellies. A finger touched that special place that she could find so readily, and in seconds Margarita arched her back, gritted her teeth, and then . . . lay still.

Julia moved up a little and wrapped both arms around Margarita. "I love you, Margarita. I will always tell you that."

She began to roll off her still enraptured lover, but Margarita stopped her. "No," she said. "Stay there."

Margarita moved her legs so that Julia's now lay between her own, and just as Julia had done, teased her until Julia was panting and biting on Margarita's neck. Margarita didn't mind. For the first time, it was completely all right that Julia was wild. There had always been the slightest of barriers that Margarita had been unable to break down in her mind — the one her mother had taught her that said nice ladies did not express such abandonment in bed. But . . . it was fine.

Julia came loudly, bringing tears to Margarita's eyes. That she could make someone else so happy. . . .

Finally Julia lifted her head from Margarita's shoulders. "Are you crying?"

"Only for joy."

Julia let out what Margarita thought was a sob as the blonde woman buried her face against Margarita's shoulder.

"And why do you cry, *amante*?"

"One day you will know, my beautiful, dark-eyed beauty."

Margarita did not understand.

As they washed the few breakfast dishes, Julia and Margarita carefully worked out the coming week. They would rest today, Sunday, and tomorrow. On Tuesday they would pick up fresh supplies. Then on Wednesday, Thursday, and Friday, they would bake. Saturday, they would go to town.

They constantly interrupted their discussions and note takings with teasing and hugs and kisses, both short ones and deep, prolonged, lingering ones that drove each other wild. An exceptionally long delay was caused by a mad chase throughout the house as Margarita tore after Julia for calling her an Anglo in disguise before Julia, howling with laughter, finally managed to yell, "You're not an Anglo, you're not an Anglo! I promise." But the promise was made only after Margarita had chased her upstairs, thrown her to the bed, and then tickled her until she could not breathe.

They slept soundly Monday night and by eight o'clock the following day, were waiting for Clare to open so that they could buy their supplies.

They were as exhausted this time as during their last baking marathon and began to bark at each other, not at all concerned with each other's feelings. They realized that their behavior was already a part of a pattern and would probably continue, that petty quarrels and snide remarks meant nothing more than it was hotter than hell in the kitchen and their feet were killing them.

By Saturday, as they drove to town, they were again the best of friends and lovers.

The two women felt mounting excitement as they drove down Colter's main street which was bustling with Saturday activity. They were sure the wagon would be empty by noon. But they never had a chance to find out because long before Julia's watch showed twelve, their wares were depleted.

Margarita was hardly able to refrain from shouting to passersby as they drove out of town, "Look what we did! We made a fortune!" Many was the compliment called to them by cowboys who had already eaten a dozen of their cookies or a lady who had enjoyed a bite of tasty cake.

Their profits this time came to fourteen dollars.

"If we do this well each time, we'll be all right," Julia said, tidying up small stacks of coins and paper dollars as she sat across the kitchen table from Margarita. "In fact, we should bake more." She glanced Margarita's way. "Will you be content?"

Margarita sat silent for some time, turning the question over very carefully in her mind. Finally she answered, "I think so."

What Julia was asking was, would she be content living with her permanently. How had it happened that she was tied to this woman — not wanting to be and yet not wanting to go? She belonged nowhere.

She did not let her upset show. "I'm tired," she said to cover a growing sense of depression. "I'm going up to take a nap."

"I'll come with you."

"No, I want to be alone." She needed solitude desperately.

"Sleep well." Julia did not try to touch her.

Margarita could have cried from the kindness in Julia's soft voice. The woman was always so understanding. It tore Margarita apart that she wasn't as sure about themselves as Julia.

She climbed the stairs with dragging feet.

Chapter Fifteen

They baked again, went to town and sold everything, this time only bringing back twelve dollars profit — not nearly enough for their time and effort. At the kitchen table, without warning, Margarita burst into uncontrollable tears, covering her face with her hands.

"Don't," Julia said softly, moving to her side and taking her in her arms. "Please don't cry. I hate it so when you're unhappy." Julia rocked her back and forth.

But Margarita could not stop crying. She asked brokenly, "What shall we do?"

"I don't know," Julia replied. "We'll talk about it. We'll make out."

"It's such a wonderful idea." Tears streamed down Margarita's face as Julia nodded in quiet agreement.

"Maybe if we worked even harder...."

But they were already doing all that they could.

"How much money do we have all together?" Julia asked.

"Thirty-six dollars." The mention of the small amount made Margarita's tears flow anew. Nine days of baking, dawn to dark, three trips to town, thirty-six paltry dollars....

"No," Julia corrected. "Not just our profits. I mean all of it. The supplies money, the emergency money, the firewood money. Every single penny."

"I don't know. Maybe eight, eighty-five dollars."

Julia was still frowning fiercely.

"Why?"

"Oh, nothing," Julia said. "Come on, let's go for a walk. We need to get away from this kitchen for a while."

Margarita awoke with a start. It was pitch black in the room. "Julia," she murmured. Margarita reached for her, only to find an empty bed. The sheets where she had lain were cool, indicating Julia had been gone for some time.

Margarita slipped out of bed and wrapped a robe around her naked body, shivering against the cold, and made her way downstairs.

By dim lantern light Julia sat hunched over the Montgomery Ward and Company catalog, leafing through its pages. She looked up with sheepish eyes. "I didn't mean to wake you."

"What are you doing?"

163

"Thinking."

"Julia, come to bed. Think in the morning."

"I can't sleep. I want to think now."

Margarita leaned over her shoulder. The Sears catalog also lay open before her. "What are you looking at tins for?"

Julia picked up the lantern and turned up the wick, brightening the room. She walked over to the oven and, bringing the lantern closer to it, began to inspect it carefully. "My father bought this cookstove for my mother years ago. He had it shopped all the way from Albany, New York. It's an I. C. Potts. I've always loved its beauty."

The name of the maker meant nothing to Margarita, but she could see that the oven was an expensive model. She hadn't seen many like it. The black beast, as the women had called it as they had sweated over it, had swinging side trivets above its six burners, with three graduated size plates designed for various degrees of heat. The stove also had a water reservoir and a warming oven. Ornate overall designs and gracefully curved legs with nickel-plated trim contrasted strikingly against its black surface.

Julia continued her detailed inspection. "It's put together with nuts and bolts and welding. If I drew a picture of every piece we took apart, where every nut and bolt went, we could put it back together ourselves if we could get a man to help us horse around the heavier parts."

"And for what purpose?"

"It would be cheaper than buying a brand new one. I'd never find one this good, used."

"You're not making sense."

"Not yet, I'm not," Julia admitted. "But in time, I will." She yawned luxuriously and put an arm around Margarita's waist. "I'm getting sleepy. Let's go to bed."

"Do you want to discuss anything?"

"No, I want to sleep."

"Immediately?"

"No."

"What do you want to do with your life? I mean really, truly do with it?" Julia lay staring at the ceiling through the dull morning grayness. Rain pelted the house, a hard tattoo on the roof.

Margarita snuggled against her almost rigid body. "So serious, first thing in the morning."

Julia glanced at her watch lying on the bedside table. "It's ten. We should have been baking since five this morning."

With a sigh, Margarita pulled away and lay beside her lover, not touching her. It seemed that Julia was going to continue her melancholy behavior. "Julia, you've been like this for five days now. When are you going to smile again? We can't bake and make a decent living at it. We know it and we've talked about it."

She couldn't go through another day with Julia staring endlessly out the window, or wandering off by herself for hours at a time. It was time to get on with things, whatever they were. "Come on. Let's get up," she said, feigning an enthusiasm she did not feel, "and start the day with a big breakfast." She pushed her lover playfully to get her going.

Julia nestled against her. "I haven't meant to be an old crab. And you're right. I've been badly discouraged.

But it hasn't all been time wasted. I've been thinking, too."

Margarita was relieved that Julia had willingly moved against her body. "What have you been thinking?"

"I asked you once what you would really like to do with your life."

Margarita burrowed deeper into Julia's sheltering arms. "I want to buy land one day. And on this land I would like to raise horses. Not scrubs, but good stock . . . already broken to the saddle and ready to be sold at a good price."

"Who would pay such a price for a good horse like that?" Julia asked casually, not even reacting to the fact that it was a novel idea for a lone woman. Perhaps not even thinking of it.

"Fort Union would."

"It would take a long time to train such a horse. He couldn't be gun-shy. He'd have to ground tie. He'd have to be fast. You'd need hired hands to help you drive the herd to the fort."

"I would do all right." Margarita spoke confidently. "I know how to breed and to train for excellent quality in a horse. I learned from Seth what and what not to do to make a good mount. Do you know," she added proudly, "that our gang's horses outran anything that came after us? Every time. Sam used to choose our horses for us. He was quite good at it."

There followed a prolonged silence as she remembered with pain her loss of the beautiful horses at the meadow. Wanting to match Julia's growing good humor, she pushed these depressing thoughts aside and asked brightly, "And you? What do you want to do?"

"I'd like to paint. I'd like to paint all day long and all night long, and never stop." Julia rolled away from Margarita and stared dreamily at the ceiling.

"Not even sometimes?" Her dark mood of a moment ago now conquered, Margarita ran her fingernails sensuously down the middle of Julia's chest and belly, and felt her shiver.

"Yes, I'd stop now and then — to eat."

"Oh, you!" Margarita squealed, and in a flash was up on her knees tickling Julia.

The desperate victim screamed in surrender, "I'd stop for you, Margarita. I would! I would!"

"All right, then," Margarita answered, laughing hard and rolling Julia over to slap her bare bottom. As they snuggled deep into the bed again, she said, "You told me painting is a chancy way to make a living."

"No doubt I'd starve."

"You have an idea, don't you?" Margarita accused, propping herself up on an elbow and looking down on her. "What is it and why haven't you talked to me about it?"

"Because I wanted to think it through first. Because the whole idea may not be sensible at all." Julia spoke earnestly. "We know we can't bake in Colter and make a living at it. But maybe we could someplace else."

Margarita tried to interrupt, but Julia stopped her with an upraised hand. "We're good cooks, Margarita. That's a fact and we've proved it all over town. I thought then that we should go someplace where there are few women. A place where, if there are any women, they're either married and busy tending a demanding man, or are ladies of the night. There would be little chance of competition then, and we could get a very good price for our goods. We could do well. Damn well."

"You're suggesting a mining town," Margarita guessed. Her eyes gleamed at this new financial possibility.

"Exactly."

"Hungry miners would pay five dollars for a pie."

"Ten," Julia corrected. "I've heard they do irrational things with their gold dust — like spend it foolishly."

"We could go down to Santa Fe. They have an assay office there. They'd know where gold strikes are happening."

"Let's ask Belle first. She may save us some time and money. She hears a lot and might know something."

"Let's go later today."

"Come on in, gals," Belle invited them loudly, waving Julia and Margarita into her receiving parlor.

Belle was small for a saloon girl, Margarita saw. Most women working in public houses had a bit more size just to protect themselves against some of the larger, rougher men who called on them. But Belle had a reputation for holding her own. Already made up for duties that would soon start in the saloon, she wore a colorful low-cut calico dress which set off her fair and freckled skin and green eyes. Long red hair was piled loosely on top of her head and her lips were painted a bright red.

Margarita looked around as she entered. In contrast to Belle's rather gaudy appearance, her receiving parlor was surprisingly restful and quiet, papered with soft shades of blue and furnished with comfortable furniture and fine rose-colored parlor lamps that sat on intricately hand-carved hardwood stands alongside the chairs and a

168

horsehair couch. She and Julia were invited to sit on the couch.

The saloon girl's living quarters were not at all what Margarita had imagined. She could have been sitting in her own parlor. There was no evidence of wild night life that would probably occur here later tonight. But then, who was she to question someone else's life? She felt guilty that she had been prepared to.

Belle said, "I want you to hear something." Proudly she cranked up and played her latest purchase from the East: a phonograph. Through its large, flower-like horn came the violin strains of *My Old Kentucky Home* and *Jeanie With The Light Brown Hair,* each melody produced from five-inch long cylinders. "See the fine grooves on this thing?" Belle asked, displaying a cylinder. "That's where the music is stored. All the time."

"Who in the world would think of such an idea?" Julia marveled.

"It says, T. A. Edison," Belle replied, reading the name off the machine.

Julia said, "I read about him in the newspaper last year. He and some other fellow, Swan, I think his name was, made the streets of New York City light up with electricity."

Incredulously Margarita asked, "How could they do that? No one can light up a whole street with electricity."

"I think they said they used glass bulbs, or something like that. I don't rightly remember. It's hard to believe, anyway."

Each cylinder was played twice more, the women thoroughly enjoying the music. Then Belle asked, "What brings you here? I don't get too many lady guests." She let out a hoarse laugh at her own joke.

Julia began her story by describing the short-lived efforts of the Blake-Sanchez baking services, concluding by briefly describing their future plans.

"A good idea, if you can do it," Belle answered enthusiastically. She relayed to her guests what she had learned not too long ago from a friendly drover, ending with, "The place is called Dimmick's Goldfield in western Arizona. It's a pretty good strike, I hear."

"Arizona is awfully far away," Julia remarked.

"You have to go where the gold is," Belle answered philosophically. "Wait here." Disappearing into another room, she returned to hand Julia a small box.

Julia and Margarita peered into the box, at a chunk of ore the size of a small fist. "Good Lord!" the women remarked simultaneously.

"That's gold," Belle said casually, "I got it six months ago from a drover who came through Colter. He won it in a card game. The man he got it from had sold his claim to somebody else. That was the only piece he'd kept, till he lost it."

"If he could find this kind of stuff," Margarita wondered as she picked up the nugget, "why did he sell out?" She hefted the gold. It lay heavy in her hand.

"The miner got twenty thousand for the claim. It was faster money than digging for it. He had a girl someplace and wanted to get rich quick and get back home even faster, as I understand the story."

Belle returned the nugget to the box. "I like to dream, so I keep the thing," she said, glancing at the container. "I'll never have much more gold than what's in that rock right there."

"How can you be sure your cowboy wasn't lying to you?" Julia asked.

"Why would he? He had nothing to gain. You can try Santa Fe if you want," Belle continued. "But I wouldn't waste my time. I'm telling you, there's a run in Dimmick's Goldfield." She spoke with assuredness.

"Then we'll make plans," Julia announced.

Margarita agreed. Belle sounded too sure to be wrong, and Julia seemed to have complete confidence in what she said. Margarita herself had heard the same strike rumors months ago from the boys after they had returned from a binge in Sourdough.

Leaving Belle's room, Julia and Margarita did not discuss their plans further, nor talk about the possibility that the dancehall girl might be mistaken. Nor did they speculate on all the things that could go wrong with the grandiose scheme that was growing and fermenting in both their minds.

By six the following morning, still in bed, they were jabbering constantly, unable to let one finish speaking before the other began.

"We'll dismantle the oven and take it with us along with every utensil in the kitchen. That'll save us quite a bit of money. We'll need a large tent to cook in. . . ."

"And to sleep in. . . ."

"We need. . . ."

Scrambling out of bed like children, they talked non-stop while they dressed.

Seated at the kitchen table, they began to compile a list of all they thought they would require to succeed, as toasted bread crumbs dribbled unnoticed to the tablecloth and coffee was swallowed in large gulps instead of leisurely lingered over.

Over the next two days, their list grew to a frightening length as they estimated goods, figured costs, and studied both the Montgomery Ward and Company and Sears,

171

Roebuck and Company catalogs for additional baking utensils. Then there was the list of people they must consult. In the end, they had assembled in the notebook a thorough inventory of bakeware and drygoods, as well as other essentials: chickens, one cow, a tent, two cots, blankets, clothing. They would need to have the wagon dismantled; it, too, would be taken along as well as the horses. The account was extensive and thorough, and it almost overwhelmed them. They agreed to set it aside for a whole day just to escape for a while the massive logistics problem looming before them.

They filled the following day by tarrying in bed until noon and taking an afternoon drive and picnic to a spot loved by Julia from her childhood, a secluded area nestled between two rolling hills. That night they made love for hours.

The next morning they arrived at a total cost, and solutions for obtaining that amount of money.

"We need five thousand, two hundred, eighty-seven dollars, and sixty-three cents. That would just set us up," Margarita said despairingly. "I *could* rob a bank."

Julia frowned. "And you *could* get yourself shot. Better that we just go borrow the money."

"You can't take a joke," Margarita pouted. Julia needn't be so serious. "I know I can't rob a bank. Not that bank."

"Not any bank," Julia warned.

"Why do you think I would even think of such an idea now?"

"Because you were a stagecoach robber — and a bank robber."

"Not a very good bank robber, but a damn good stagecoach robber."

"Never mind. We will borrow the money."

"With my way, we wouldn't owe money."

"You can forget your way. Even if you did get away with such an act, it would likely take more than a single robbery to gain five thousand dollars."

Margarita looked questioningly at Julia. "You've thought about it . . . about robbery . . . haven't you?" She could barely contain herself. "Now you understand why one might become an outlaw. The rewards come fast."

"Not fast enough, Yellowthroat. We'll go to the bank tomorrow — and borrow."

Julia's pronouncement, which Margarita knew was the only possible solution, caused a brief but painful nostalgia within her. It had been a very free life she had once led in spite of tough men and crude living conditions. No, she told herself firmly, this life was better — and she would allow herself to think no more about the past.

Chapter Sixteen

The following morning at nine o'clock, Margarita and Julia were at the Colter Bank. One of the tellers politely escorted them into the private office of President Douglas B. Marsh who stood to greet them. Margarita hid her hands in the folds of her dress to conceal their shaking. This place always made her nervous.

Margarita was introduced. The banker had known Julia since she was a little girl. She had tended his wife and children from time to time when they had needed medical help or something from the drugstore's shelves.

Marsh's office was neat and precisely furnished. Shelves of books occupied two walls, a painting of his family dominated another. A large mahogany desk, graced by three expensive leather chairs, seemed to fill the room.

Marsh looked a bit like a giant, the impression partially created by a massive head with thick, unruly silver hair. His face was half hidden behind a luxurious mustache and generous muttonchops. Deep blue eyes pierced anyone who looked into them. A gold chain hung across the vest of an expensive black suit; Marsh's thumbs, on surprisingly slender hands, were hooked in the tiny pockets of the vest, holding back his coat and revealing a spreading waistline.

He gestured for the women to be seated. Settling his large frame behind the desk, he leaned back comfortably. "Good to see you again, Julia. Wonderfully tasty pie you baked last week. My wife told me that when I saw you I was to order another right away."

Margarita waited impatiently while Julia smiled and exchanged banalities with Marsh for five minutes. She wanted to conclude this discussion quickly and get out of here. Holding her handbag tightly with both hands to hide their continued trembling, she ignored the sweat dampening her underarms.

Julia finally spoke in earnest. "I have an idea I would like to propose to you, Douglas." She withdrew the notebook from her purse and painstakingly explained their plans. Marsh listened with acute attention. She spoke confidently as if she had been to Dimmick's Goldfield, had studied the area personally, and knew to a body how many people were already at the fields.

Then Julia told him the exact amount that she and Margarita wished to borrow. Marsh smiled slightly,

175

relaying a ray of optimism to Margarita that he would lend them the money without question.

"Well," Marsh finally said, after he had sat a full minute in silence. "That is an ambitious undertaking, isn't it? I can see you've given it a lot of thought." He laced thin fingers together across his paunch. "But you must realize, ladies, that it's an impossible thing you ask."

His words struck Margarita like a hammer blow. She hadn't realized how much hope she had placed on this man.

"I don't understand," Julia said.

"The whole idea is quite preposterous," he said. "Two women going off alone into unknown territory."

"There are seven thousand people in Dimmick's right now, and the place is still growing rapidly," Margarita declared. "That can hardly be considered the unknown." She could back Julia's facts, whether she knew them to be true or not.

Marsh held up a condescending hand. "It's a place full of tough men. Gamblers, miners, speculators . . . like yourselves."

"And women — some wives," Julia added. "An established community."

"Hardly." Marsh leaned forward and rested his arms on his desk. "Frankly, I don't loan money to women, Julia. I never have. I thought you understood that."

"No, I do not understand that," she replied sharply. "I have never heard it mentioned in Colter."

"Oh, yes. A few women have been to see me. I've had to turn them down."

"Had to? Why? Women earn money. This town has had several women proprietors — and a female lawyer."

"And they give the money they earn to their husbands, who, in turn, put it in my bank. And I take careful care of it for the ladies."

"Through their husbands."

"Exactly right. A woman's head is unable to deal with large figures."

"So, what you're saying is that a woman may save here — preferably through her husband, but she cannot borrow."

"Precisely."

"Oh, stop using big words like some damn Easterner, Douglas," Julia snapped. "You used to stomp through cow shit in the fields just like my father did."

Margarita watched Marsh's ears turn red. If the situation were not so humorless she would have burst out laughing.

"I'm not your run-of-the-mill woman, Douglas," Julia stated. "You know that that money you speak of is still in your vault because of me."

"Why? Because you painted the picture on the wall?" He glared at her with his piercing eyes.

"This bank has never lost as much as one penny due to that painting. It was a grand plan."

"Yes, that's true, Julia," Marsh readily agreed. "A grand plan, indeed." The banker removed a slim cigar from inside his coat pocket and carefully snipped off one end with a tiny gold pocket-knife. Lighting it, he blew a lazy puff of thin, blue smoke toward the ceiling. "But I must remind you," he said, studying its glowing end, "it was a man, a member of the town council, who thought up the idea."

"Oh, posh!" Julia exploded. "It was my fine work that stopped thieves so successfully."

Julia's blunt honesty stung Margarita. But she listened with growing hatred of Marsh and his down-the-nose attitude toward the two of them, toward women in general. If only she dared tell him just who she was. She would put the fear of a bandito into his heart. Yellowthroat would destroy him.

Marsh reached across his desk and knocked ash into a small clean ashtray. "You force me to repeat myself, Julia. It was a man's idea. You merely followed orders."

"Orders!" she exclaimed. "Orders! I was asked, not ordered, as the only artist in Colter, if I would do it. I didn't even request payment."

"We did buy your paints for you," Marsh said kindly.

Rolling her eyes toward the ceiling, Margarita could not help saying spitefully, "Oh, how incredibly generous."

Julia gave her a sharp look. "What about all the business my father transacted at this bank for years and years?" she asked Marsh. "Doesn't that count for something? Can't you see that I am his daughter? That I would not shame his name by incurring a bad debt? Perhaps I could mortgage my home."

"I'm sorry, Julia. It's the bank's policy not to lend money to women." He turned to Margarita. "I'm very sorry, Madam."

"A moment ago it was *your* policy, Mr. Marsh, not to grant loans to women," Margarita said in a near shaking voice. Her head ached viciously. "Just exactly whose policy is it? Yours personally, or the bank's?" This man no longer made her nervous. He made her angry.

"I speak for the bank, Madam," he said, his eyes boring into hers.

Margarita did not yield to his fixed stare, but she tightened her hands in her lap and clenched her teeth, not

178

daring to speak further lest she say something to draw undesirable attention to herself. Abruptly, she stood. "Are you ready, Julia?"

"Quite," came the crisp reply.

Marsh, too, began to rise to see them out.

"Oh, don't bother to get up, Douglas," Julia said, stopping him midway with a raised palm. "We know where the door is . . . as do all women who come to you for help. And please watch. Notice how capable I am of opening this door unassisted." She swung wide the door and exited with sweeping grace. Margarita, her nose high in the air, followed and did not look back.

The two women walked decisively through the bank and out its front doors. Still holding their heads high, they climbed into the buggy.

Before Julia could bring the buggy around, Belle walked up to them. "Howdy, girls. Get your loan?"

"Oh, hello, Belle." Julia glanced briefly at her friend and shook her head.

"What's the problem?"

"He said he would never loan money to women. Any woman."

"He said that? Why, that perfect piece of prairie dog shit." Belle's angry voice caused Julia and Margarita to look keenly at her. "Listen, gals, you go right back into that bank. Knock down the damn door to get into his office if you have to, and stay there. I'll be right over."

"What are you talking about?"

"You want to go to Dimmick's Goldfield, don't you?"

"Of course we do," they chimed.

"Then do what I tell you, and don't let him throw you out." Then Belle suddenly asked, "How about taking me along? I could use a change of scenery."

"I don't mind, do you, Margarita?" Julia asked, turning to her.

"Not at all," Margarita readily agreed.

"Belle," Julia said, "it's a long hard trip. Why —"

"I'll do the same thing there that I'm doing right here — only make more money at it," the saloon girl answered with a laugh. "Maybe I could help you during the day — if I have any energy left. Don't know why I didn't think of it before now. I'll come back rich as a queen. Maybe even start my own house."

"Why would you want to come back to Colter?" Margarita questioned her, gesturing at the town with contempt.

"Why not? I've been here so long it's home now. Besides, it'll give the ladies something to talk about for years at their quilting bees." She chuckled lightly to herself. "You go on back to the bank now. I'll be along. Remember, don't let him throw you out." She hastened toward the saloon.

"Well, life is funny, isn't it?" Margarita remarked.

Julia shrugged. "Let's go and see just how funny."

A few minutes later the two women sat firmly anchored to the chairs they had recently vacated, while a blustering, red-faced Marsh stood at the open door of his office trying to shoo them out.

"I already explained, Julia, and very patiently, I might add, that I don't loan money to women."

"You do now," came a commanding voice. Belle breezed through the door.

"Belle!"

"Hello, Douglas," Belle said with a smile. "Why don't you just shut the door and let's rehash this whole thing?"

"I don't want any interruptions, Abner," he called to the nearest teller. "None." He closed the door and pulled up an extra chair for Belle. "What's this all about?" he demanded, seating himself behind the desk. "How did you get involved, Belle? I already told these women that the bank doesn't loan —"

"Yes, yes, yes," Belle interrupted. "They explained. Now let me spell out something very clearly to you, Douglas. You are going to give them the money. How much is it, Julia?" A graceful hand patted her already neat hair.

Julia read from her notepad. "Five thousand two hundred and eighty-seven dollars and sixty-three cents."

"You're going to give them five thousand two hundred eighty-seven dollars and sixty-three cents," Belle said. "In fact. . . ." She suggested to the two women, "You'd better have him add another thousand to that. Give yourselves a little room to breathe. In addition," she said, turning back to Marsh. "I'll be leaving with them."

"You can't."

"Why on earth not?"

"Because, because. . . ."

"I understand, Douglas," Belle said. "But as you know, things — and people — change. And obviously you have changed."

With great interest and growing amusement Margarita watched the nervous, fidgeting banker and the extremely confident saloon girl.

Marsh remained firm. "I still will not loan the money."

Belle cocked her head to one side. "Are you absolutely sure?"

"Yes!"

Unruffled by his vehemence, the saloon girl reached into her purse and pulled out a small blue sheet of paper. Leaning toward Julia, she sniffed at it. "Scented, you

181

know." She began to read. "My darling sugar plum. I can't begin to tell you how much I've missed —"

"Sugar plum?" Julia quickly said, an understanding smile crossing her face.

Marsh leaped from his chair. "I won't be blackmailed," he thundered. He slammed a fist on his highly polished desk.

Belle looked up innocently from the note. Marsh's face was purple with fury. The only sound in the room was the ticking of the clock on the wall and his labored breathing. Unmoved, she glanced again at the note and continued reading. ". . . how much I've missed you since last night when —"

"*Damn* your ungrateful hide, you blackmailing little whore!" The banker mopped a perspiring forehead.

"Your wife would love to have this. It's even dated and signed. Probably a banker's habit." She leaned toward Julia and pointed at the signature. "And the jewelry. It's really quite beautiful."

"You swore you'd burn —"

"My God, Douglas, a girl's got to have some protection against the men in her life. You demand collateral daily right here in this bank. Why would you think I would do less in my line of work?"

"All right, then! Six thousand two hundred and eighty-seven dollars."

"And sixty-eight cents."

"And sixty-eight cents," Marsh roared. "And not a penny more! And I'll be damned glad never to see you again."

The dancehall girl smiled, but kept still.

Julia said, "Kindly deposit the money in a joint account for us now, Douglas." She held out her hand, palm up. "And we'd like a receipt."

"And don't you dare stand in their way, darlin'," Belle warned. "Or I'll send your wife —"

"You're biting off your nose to spite your face, Belle. What're they to you?" He jerked his shaggy head toward his newest clients. "I gave you good money. What the hell have they done for you?"

"The difference is, Douglas, that they see me as a human being. You only see me as a whore."

"You women are all alike." Marsh steadied himself against the edge of his desk, his face a dangerous red. "A conniving, scheming, bunch of hellcats."

"Of course we are," the saloon girl agreed cheerfully. "How do you think we've gotten as far as we have? You're a user, Douglas. That's all you've ever been. You really should have helped them." Standing, Belle turned her attention toward her friends. "He'll have the money for you in a few minutes, ladies. Come and see me afterward. We'll have breakfast over at Nancy's Restaurant and celebrate." She walked to the door. Her hand on the knob, she turned to Marsh. "You know, honey, you never were that good in bed. But, oh, the money you laid on my table. It made it all worthwhile." She slammed the door. Her perfume lingered in the air behind her.

Margarita and Julia each stifled a smirk as Marsh stood, visibly trembling, staring at the closed door. He glared at them. "A word of this to my wife. . . ."

"You may rely on our discretion," Julia promised.

Chapter Seventeen

Margarita and Julia could not go to Dimmick's Goldfield for some months. The necessity to find someone to rent the house, waiting for mail orders to arrive from the East, for shipment of the oven, wagon, and stock, and all the additional equipment they would take along took weeks; too many weeks to think that going to Dimmick's at this late time in the year would be a practical move.

It was an opportunity for Margarita to insist that Julia teach her to read. Using the Bible and the weekly newspaper, Margarita learned to cope with English relatively well. She followed with interest the news of America's growing railroads through Canada and across this vast country down to old Mexico, and of the new games mentioned in the women's section called tennis and bingo, and that canned meats as well as fruits were becoming more popular in stores now. She wondered if there would come a day when women would no longer put food by, but simply go to the store and buy what they needed. She read about the continued deterioration of the United States' president, James Garfield, since being shot this past July by Charles Jules Guiteau, a disgruntled office seeker. It was reported that Garfield had blood poisoning and was in a great deal of pain. In an October paper, she read to Julia in halting English that he had died on the nineteenth of September. She had been watching his progress so closely for so many days that she was unable to read the words without feeling sadness for the man.

Margarita and Julia stayed in Colter until the early spring of 1882, spending the time in further planning, having the wagon dismantled, fattening up their horses for God only knew what, buying a cow — and learning how to milk her — and how to shovel shit in record time because they both despised cleaning out the stall in the barn where she was spending the winter; learning all about chickens — and learning to hate them, too; and gathering together all the goods that arrived by train and through the mails. There were tins for pies, cakes, cookies, and bread, and metal plateware, because glass or bakeware might not survive the journey, and a gun or two — just in case; and other needed implements such as needles, thread, razor-sharp knives; a tent, cots, more lanterns and blankets and linens. The supplies piled up in the parlor and spilled over into the kitchen, and throughout the cold season it felt like Christmas.

Owning the cow and chickens had added a bonus. Margarita and Julia made a little extra money throughout the winter selling their milk and eggs to Clare at the Emporium. There had been, too, some relief for the Sanchez family in Mexico from part of the bank loan sent them through the United States Mail Office.

Then came the day when the last box had been packed and hauled to the train station and the final dusting of the house done so that the new renters would not think Julia a poor housekeeper.

Margarita and Julia drank a cup of coffee heated over a small fire outdoors because the oven was already crated and waiting at the station. The renters would have to supply their own cookstove. They drank coffee in haste and nervousness as they waited for Belle to pick them up in a rented two-seat buggy. Their animals had been taken to the blacksmith's stable the day before. They, too, would be waiting at the station, brought there by the smithy.

The women were edgy as they washed and dried the dishes and put them neatly away. One at a time, they ran to the backhouse for a quick stop. At last they were ready. The house was ready. The time had come.

"Hello, the house!" came a shout from outside.

"Let's go," Julia said.

Staring into each other's eyes, they gave one another a hard, almost desperate hug.

"Well, Yellowthroat?"

"Well, *artista*?"

Julia locked up and hung the key on a nail by the door. They looked back once as the buggy pulled away, and then they rode down the road toward Colter as if they hadn't a care in the world.

In five or ten minutes the conductor would yell, "Broken—wiiing!" signaling Julia and Margarita and Belle to depart the train and see to it that their animals and endless boxes and barrels of goods were transferred and packed carefully onto the waiting bullwhackers' ox-drawn carts that would take them and their supplies the final ninety miles north through the mountain passes to Dimmick's Goldfield.

The women had spent the last five days and four nights riding second class on dusty trains, first traveling north on the Union Pacific to the Colorado border, then switching to the Atchison, Topeka & Santa Fe, before final boarding onto the Southern Pacific, down in Tucson.

They took turns napping on the single bench to which they were entitled while the other two women sat up. They had brought along canned and dried foods, eating nutritiously but unimaginatively, and drinking tepid water offered by the conductor. They were uncomfortable but remained in high spirits, with the bulk of their conversation centering on the money they thought they could make in the next few months; more, they estimated, than they could earn in two, perhaps three years, had they stayed in Colter, or moved to another town, and baked.

On the second day of their journey the train made a prolonged stop in Santa Fe. The three women left the train long enough to enjoy an outstanding noonday meal at a restaurant located next to the station house. Harvey Girls, all dressed alike with dark brown dresses protected by snow white aprons reaching from bosom to floor, brought them course after delicious course of game birds and fish, boiled potatoes, several fresh vegetables, sweet cakes, and coffee. The women could barely rise from the table to make the short return trip back to the train depot.

From Colter to Dimmick's, more than eight hundred miles away, the land changed and then changed again from gentle, rolling, grassy hills to high craggy mountains and mesas hundreds of feet high, and monstrous cliffs streaked with hues of reds and browns and rusts. The train rolled across great frightening gorges and onto shrub-covered plains interrupted by rugged mountains, slab-sided buttes, and occasional sand dunes. Just before the train reached Tucson, it passed through the giant multi-armed saguaro, abundant as trees in a forest, some as much as fifty feet high and weighing up to ten tons, and kept company by the low prickly pear cactus. Bright flowers of red and yellow and gold splashed in undulating waves of color across the desert floor.

Before they reached Brokenwing, the women had forgotten where they had seen this gorge or that mountain, or the beautiful eagle soaring in the sky, so much had they observed.

At each station change they were worried sick that their precious belongings would not be handled well, that their livestock would not be able to tolerate the long journey, that their luggage and supplies would be lost or stolen or destroyed. They hovered around the baggage handlers who moved their animals and supplies. Their collective worry was intense but unnecessary. Every article and creature they owned, with the exception of two hens — good layers they were, too — make it to Brokenwing, the place where all those continuing north to Dimmick's Goldfield must depart the train.

On the fifth day the train screeched to a halt at a waterstop at the northern edge of the Sonoran Desert where cactus — spiny teddy bear chollas — marched across the land by the thousands. Exiting their car, the women looked around tentatively. Even Margarita, who had traveled hundreds of miles alone across open territory, felt intimidated by the hostility of the country. Unconsciously she moved closer to Julia.

The bullwhackers were the only ones to greet the departing passengers. They had met this train dozens of times, their wagons with teams of fourteen or more oxen standing stoically in the afternoon sun, awaiting the newest arrivals from all over the country. The bullwhackers would make money today. It was pay up or carry your load on your back. The travelers would quickly learn that from now on nothing was cheap.

Patiently the bullwhackers waited to see who unloaded the most boxes and barrels and other crated bundles ready for hauling. The more bundles, the more money. Other travelers stepped off the train and headed immediately for Dimmick's on foot with only what they could carry on their backs. Some shouted and hooted, others whistled nameless tunes, high spirited as they headed north. In about a day's time, the walkers, footsore and exhausted, would be passed by the wagoners. The bullwhackers would pick up additional dollars hauling these tired bodies without taxing the oxen at all, their animals more precious to the drivers than anything else they owned. It was a lucrative trade, making the whackers richer, faster, than most miners would ever become.

There were no baggage handlers here. Brokenwing barely counted as a whistle-stop. And so for an hour three dozen men and the three women unloaded the train, stacks of goods to go to Dimmick's Goldfield rising higher and higher beneath the afternoon sun. Even in the heat, people laughed and called to each other, the men joking

189

about beginning a new town altogether, what with all the things they had brought along.

Indeed, some were here to try to do exactly that — if the gold lasted long enough. More and better saloons would be built, and more bath houses; a Bible-thumper, the first preacher to be going to Dimmick's, had brought along boxes of Bibles, and was promising to build a church this summer. One gentleman had for the five days gone from one end to the other of the fifteen-car train, loudly bragging about his drugs and perfumes. If he couldn't cure folks, they'd go out smellin' pretty.

Most of those aboard the train were serious business people. They had carefully calculated every necessary item to bring, had done their research, just as Julia and Margarita and Belle had. They were glad to see tough looking guards standing by the bullwhackers' wagons, holding shotguns and rifles as if they were part of their bodies.

Finally the train was emptied of its enterprisers and their possessions. A lonesome whistle screamed across the desert as the train began to chug slowly toward the west, continuing its long journey, leaving the newest residents of Dimmick's Goldfield gazing after it, some apprehensively, some completely unconcerned, some already wishing they were at the fields, set up, and raking in gold hand over fist.

The women were of the group who looked with apprehension after the train. "We will make it," Margarita said determinedly. "We didn't come here to fail."

"Of course we didn't," Julia answered confidently. "Let's get us a wagon."

Someone behind them said, "Help you, ladies?" They turned with surprise toward the female voice.

Five and a half feet tall, a slim woman in a plain brown dress trimmed with a wide white collar walked over to them, her skirt carving a soft pattern in the dust as it trailed slightly behind her. She carried a heavy stick in one weatherworn hand, and in the other a bullwhip which she gently slapped against her leg. "Name's Arizona Mary." Her face was heavily tanned and her intensely blue eyes crinkled at the corners with mirth. White teeth sparkled in her dark face. She wore a sunbonnet covering brown hair tucked loosely beneath.

"Come again?" Julia asked.

"Arizona Mary."

How did we miss seeing her, Margarita wondered.

Mary thrust out a wide brown palm with thick short fingers, shaking each woman's hand. With interest, Margarita noted the roughness of the palm. The only other woman's hand she knew that felt like that was her own, no longer as rough since being so long away from the meadow.

"Mind doin' business with a woman?"

Wide-eyed, Margarita asked, "Is this your wagon? Are these your oxen?"

"All fourteen of 'em. All paid for. You wanna ship with me?"

Their hesitation must have caused the slim bullwhacker concern, for she quickly said, "I can cuss with the best of 'em."

Out of the corner of her eye, Margarita saw another bullwhacker approach.

Mary looked toward the advancing man. "I can give you a better deal."

"You *are* a better deal, Arizona Mary!" Julia spoke quickly. "I'm sure your rates are fair. Let's load."

191

Carelessly Mary flipped the whip onto the seat of the tall wagon. "I'll help you. Let's go." Without a word, the man turned back and approached another group who waited by their own small mountain of belongings.

"Looks like you made him angry," Margarita said.

"Oh, that's old Jessie. Him and me are always stealin' from each other. Keeps us on our toes. You load, I direct," she said briskly. "Whackers don't load. Git the weight in the middle. Keep everything even on both sides. Don't leave any gaps in between boxes." She climbed onto the seat and continued to guide from there, advising the travelers on how to properly build their stack, occasionally having the grunting and sweating women reposition a box here or a barrel there, for better weight distribution.

It took over two hours to pack, tie the cow and horses to the rear of the wagon, and settle themselves and the chickens, housed in three large bar crates, on top of the freight. They had paid a man thirty dollars to help unload the oven from the train. It had cost another thirty to get it onto the wagon.

"Just hang on tight if you get to rockin' too bad," Mary advised, and with surprisingly powerful lungs yelled "Gitup, ox," following the command with a long string of curses and a sharp crack of her bullwhip that snapped over the backs of the big rusty colored beasts, never touching their hides. Other voices of bullwhackers sounded out. Grunts and snorts from the oxen filled the air as they strained against their yokes. Almost as one, the line of wagons began to creak and groan in protest under their staggering weight as they began to roll northward.

"I can't believe we brought enough to fill this entire wagon," Belle said.

192

"We brought it all," Julia answered, and grabbed a rope securing the canvas on which they sat as the vehicle hit a stone in the path they now traveled.

It wasn't long before Belle said, "I'm getting down to walk. This is too rough for me."

The others agreed, and climbed gingerly to the ground to walk alongside the wide iron-rimmed wheels rather than be unpleasantly jolted about.

As they walked, they chatted with Mary. She had been a bullwhacker for years, she told them. Couldn't bear being inside a house. But she was a lady, mind you. Wore a dress ever' day she worked. In turn, her customers told her their stories, relaying their dreams, asking her opinion. "You'll do well. The men will eat anything, and if it's sweet, they'll eat ten times as much. An' they're always lookin' fer more entertainment."

While en route, they contracted with Arizona Mary to freight future supplies, quickly sealing the bargain with a down payment of three hundred dollars hard cash before they even knew for certain what they would need.

She had already been paid four hundred dollars to take them to Dimmick's. Not expecting the cost to be that high, they were glad now that Belle had suggested they borrow the extra thousand.

The eight wagons traveled until seven that evening. The passengers were happy to stop. The miles they had walked or ridden had been long and exhausting. Sitting around a campfire and drinking coffee and eating beans and biscuits was the only thing they had thought about for the last two hours. No one had expected to travel this late today.

The supplies required for cooking and sleeping had been logically packed last: pots, pans, food, bed rolls. A few curses by greenhorns who had not thought ahead could be heard throughout the quiet camp as they shifted boxes to reach what they needed.

At a stream near a small hill, thirsty animals lapped up silvery water. A heavy oak bucket in her hand, Margarita carried the delicious fluid back to camp and set it down carefully by Belle who had volunteered to be first to cook. Margarita wiped the sweat from her brow with the back of her hand and dried it against her skirt. "Damn, it's hot for spring," she said, and offered a big dipperful of water to Julia who smiled a grateful thanks. A disgruntled Belle took the second dipperful and said, "Try cookin'," a bead of sweat clinging precariously to the tip of her nose.

Belle was right. Margarita shouldn't have even mentioned the heat. She didn't have to sit before a fire stirring beans and baking biscuits. She thought, as her mouth puckered involuntarily, that they could eat dried foods for tomorrow's meals. She gave up the idea instantly. After a day's walk on the trail or riding on top of that rocking wagon, none of them would want to eat leather food. She herself would cook for them all tomorrow and keep still about it.

At the end of the day, guards were posted around the wagons as the passengers crawled beneath. They rolled themselves in blankets and in minutes were asleep.

It was the fifth night that Margarita and Julia hadn't slept together. Margarita missed feeling Julia lying in her arms, a leg thrown carelessly across her as her lover breathed deeply and contentedly.

She wondered why she even thought about it, why she cared so much. All along she had known that one day she would be leaving. She could not see herself a year, two years, five years down the line, still living with Julia. Julia had been so strong-minded about her staying, coming right out and telling her that was what she wanted, that she, Margarita, had gone along with the idea, not wanting to hurt her. It would be very hard now to be truthful, but she would do it all the same. It was just a matter of an appropriate moment. It would be after she had all the money she needed, free at last, to rebuild her life. Meanwhile she would continue on as if nothing were changed.

She fell into a troubled, restless sleep. Her thoughts became so real that she seemed to already miss Julia's touch. She would be glad when Julia finally knew what was on her mind.

For thirteen days the bullwhackers hauled them northward, beginning at seven each morning, nooning at watering holes or streams, and then continuing on until five in the afternoon, winding deeper and deeper through mountain passes and rich forests.

We'll be there tomorrow," one hoary bullwhacker promised the tired travelers who had gathered together as a group on this final night for supper. They had all come to know one another on the trail and last evening had agreed to eat as a family. The men treated the ladies with respect, promising the future bakers of Dimmick's Goldfield to sample their wares as soon as they were set up.

That evening after supper Belle said, "I'll be gone for a while. Don't wait up for me."

"I wonder where she's going," Julia commented as Belle walked away.

"To work, *pogo*," Margarita answered, and tucked the last of the dishes into a box, placing it beside their wagon for immediate use in the morning.

"Wonder what she'll charge?"

"Plenty, if she's smart. We're in gold country."

"She'll make more than we've made so far."

"A dollar an egg and three dollars for a quart of milk isn't bad, Julia."

"Still, she does have the advantage, doesn't she? We have to milk twice a day; stick our hands into those wretched chicken cages daily. I hate it. For her, five, ten minutes, and she's a hundred dollars richer, or ought to be."

"Our way is better." Margarita knew what she was talking about. She had sold herself many times for information. As it turned out, not a moment of it had been worth her time.

That night Julia and Margarita rolled themselves into their blankets as the last of the light fell, looking only at each other. They hadn't as much as exchanged a passing caress since they had arrived at Brokenwing; not even during a normal day's activities. This was not only gold country, it was also man's country, and they were prudent and cautious.

It would be nice when they could once again sleep in privacy, even it was to be only a lowly tent.

Chapter Eighteen

"Dimmick's," Julia said breathlessly.

The day was brilliant, the air pure and cool. Only birds decorated the cloudless sky. In fact, many birds, Margarita noted. Big birds. Buzzards, she realized. Why buzzards?

The guards had gotten everyone up earlier than usual this morning. There were only a few miles left to go, but the bullwhackers wanted to be there by nine in order to begin their return trip to the train that in another two weeks would be coming from the west with new passengers.

Arizona Mary's wagon was last today. She had started the trip first in line nearly two weeks ago, each day the lead wagon dropping back to the rear, the second wagon then becoming first, so that no one had to eat dust all the time. But even the dust did not dampen the hopeful travelers' spirits as they rode high on the wagon to see Dimmick's.

As they crested a rise to begin their final long, slow descent to town, Margarita stared with sickened disbelief at what had drawn the buzzards to the area.

A thousand memories assaulted her, wrenching her back to that time when her world had been ripped to shreds. She could not tear her eyes away from the distant scene. She knew with ghastly horror that men would never change, never be kind, never be gentle. And even as she admitted this to herself, she felt defeated with the knowledge that one day she would marry again, would have to marry. She could not live alone. Not for the rest of her life. She would become the wife of a man who was capable of doing this to another human being.

They were upon the scene now. The tree was big. The biggest in the area. They must have forced the unfortunate victims to stand on a wagon seat to get them this high. Even in the still air, the bodies rotated slowly. They had not been blindfolded and their eyes protruded horridly from their faces. Their skin color was as gray as slate, and their necks were grotesquely long and taut as the weight of their bodies pulled against the thick rope that had ended their lives. Around each neck hung a sign whitewashed with a single word:

CLAMEJUMPER

"Why, ain't that Josh 'n Andrew?" Mary called to the driver ahead of her.

"Shore looks it, don't it?" he yelled back.

"Them boys knew better." Mary's wagon creaked loudly as it rolled by the grisly scene.

For the first time since they had boarded the train in Colter, Julia touched her, putting a supporting and comforting arm around her lover. She and Belle helped the weak-kneed and nauseous Margarita down off the wagon, keeping her between them as she walked off old memories and a deep emotional wound. She had never dreamed she would see a hanging again.

"Why do they do such things?" Margarita asked. "Why? We marry them, live with them, raise their children. And yet. . . ." Tears streamed unashamedly down her face.

"That's why I take them for all they're worth," Belle answered. "I made seventy dollars the other night and only laid with two of them, and them not even bullwhackers. They thought they were real men, but I can fake it. Oh, I can fake it."

"What in hell is a real man," Julia demanded, "if they do that to each other?" She gestured with her head toward the dead men.

"I don't know," Belle answered. "I feel sorry for them all. But," she added, "they're going to make me rich."

Feeling more in control, Margarita shrugged off the women's hands. "I'm fine now. Thank you." But she wasn't fine. She knew what the future held for her. She didn't relish it. She wished her husband were alive. He had been kind. And, she staunchly told herself, she had loved him. Very much. Determined to arrive in Dimmick's with a smile on her face no matter how she was still

199

feeling inside, she said firmly, "A new life. Let's begin it with happiness."

"Let's," Julia answered stoutly, and Belle began to lead the rest of the way on foot.

A half mile from the edge of town, Julia said, "Stop here, Mary. This is where we'll live."

The three women stood quietly. Ahead of them lay Dimmick's Goldfield. In two single rows creating a main street were buildings of crude lumber with whitewashed signs — businesses which had been thrown together in haste last year for those rugged souls who sought to stay the winter. Strewn in haphazard fashion, dozens of tents dotted the surrounding area. There was a cemetery off to the right of town, clearly visible on a rise of ground, its more than two dozen graves marked with nameless crosses.

Rough garbed men, and horses, mules, and wagons filled the street. A heavy rain had hit the area two nights ago. On the trail, everyone had huddled beneath wagons. Here, there had been buildings and tents to escape within, but runoff had turned the ground to a mucky yellow soil. Mud sucked at boots and hooves and wagon wheels, while shouting men cursed the animals, the mire, and each other. Along with this noise, Margarita counted tunes from three different pianos and gunshots from two different directions.

As the din filled their ears, each woman stood lost in thought of her life ahead until the end of summer. It would be a long season.

"Come on, ladies," Arizona Mary said. "Git the wagon unloaded."

And they obeyed; box after box, barrel after barrel, crate after crate. Again, Julia paid to have the oven moved. This time the cost was fifty dollars for the added

200

help. The cow and horses were tied to a crate, and the hens, at last set free, began to squawk and to scratch and peck at the ground and to beat their wings wildly.

Belle had learned from Arizona Mary that there were five women of the night in town, and a man had to wait days to visit one. He didn't mind handing over gold dust for her favors. She didn't mind taking it. Now three more ladies had arrived.

The day's idle miners walked over to greet the bullwhackers' wagons. Seeing Arizona Mary's freight, the men cried out happily, "Thanks Mary." No one bothered making overtures to her. She was a bullwhacker — that was all.

Other men were already propositioning the new arrivals. "We're bakers," Julia announced loudly and firmly, pointing to both herself and Margarita.

"I'm not," Belle said. She only had to tell them once and the men left Julia and Margarita to fight for the right to talk to the dancehall girl. The throng quickly thickened around her but no one touched her. "Come back tomorrow," she shouted to them. "Right here. Then we can talk — if that's what you really want to do." They shouted and hooted and slapped their knees at her wit. But they didn't go away.

If the men didn't go away, they at least backed off, giving the ladies room to set up their camps. Two men put the oven together under Julia's watchful eye. It had been decided to leave it outside, thirty or so feet away from the tent for safety's sake. If it rained, there would be no baking. If it didn't, there would. As much as the oven meant to Julia, it would be sold in the fall, so rusting was of little concern to her. She promised the laborers the first pie for their efforts, and they raised a rumpus until Belle couldn't stand it anymore and walked over from her site to tell them to settle down or not bother coming back for their pie — or for her.

All that day the women worked. First they opened the boxes that held the tents. They had practiced pitching them last fall when they had come in from Ward's, and their experience now allowed them to raise the tents with a minimum of difficulty. The shelters were big and heavy and bulky, the thick canvas fighting their hands as they pulled and tugged on ropes, drawing the sides and tops taut, and tying the structures down to stakes driven deep into the ground with a sledge hammer that yanked at their back muscles with every swing.

They moved the rest of their belongings inside, first opening boxes outdoors, then packing their contents within. It would be days before they were completely organized, and they fought off waves of depression as they became more and more tired and the long day wore on, as the sun dipped closer and closer to the horizon.

They moved between each other's tenting areas, helping one another and offering words of encouragement. It was three o'clock before Belle's shelter was up and her things stashed away. Compared to Margarita's and Julia's tent, Belle's took no time at all to make ready; her furniture was crates and boxes, her bed a single wide cot. There were piles of sheets and blankets — she knew she would need plenty of those.

At five, Margarita and Julia were finished, and flopped down on two of the empty crates littering the surrounding area. The sound of both their stomachs rumbling simultaneously sent them into peals of near hysterical laughter. "I think we'd better eat," Margarita suggested, wiping away tears. "I believe we are completely exhausted."

"Or mad," Julia added.

202

In thirty minutes all three relaxed before an open fire, eating beans, salted bacon, and boiled potatoes. Occasionally small knots of men would stop by to see how they were doing, offering helpful comments and suggestions and sharing a pot of fresh strong coffee.

By nine that night, beneath woolen blankets that kept them comfortably warm and snug, the women slept soundly on hard canvas cots.

Margarita awoke with a start. She didn't move, not even to open her eyes. She concentrated solely on the sound that had disturbed her, using old talents as a tracker to determine what was happening. In the tent's blackness, the noise seemed to be near the door. Cautiously she looked in that direction. A narrow slit of barely discernible light appeared as the flap was stealthily drawn back.

From beneath her blanket she withdrew a gun, pointed it at the crack and cocked the hammer. The noise seemed louder than a gunshot. The light disappeared; footsteps receded rapidly into the night.

Margarita called Julia's name softly, but she slept soundly on. Deciding not to disturb her, Margarita sat up and swung her feet over the edge of the bed. She would stand watch the rest of the night.

At first light, Julia opened her eyes. Margarita sat straight and rigid on her cot, wide awake and watchful. Julia looked at the gun in the small woman's hand. "What's going on?"

"We had a night caller. A hen is missing. Otherwise everything is all right."

"How's Belle?"

"Still sleeping. She must not have heard him."

"We must hire a guard today."

Mutely, Margarita agreed.

They ate breakfast quickly, then headed for Dimmick's, leaving Belle to sleep. Before they had gone twenty feet, mud covered their shoes and dirtied the bottoms of their dresses. Without complaint they continued on.

They stopped at the first saloon they came to, already in full swing. Howls and whistles greeted them as they entered. Something crunched beneath Margarita's feet and she looked down to see peanut shells scattered everywhere; thousands of discarded tobacco butts and shells had turned the floor a rich brown color, and endless traffic had beaten it into a granite-hard surface. Stale tobacco, thick cigar smoke, and pungent whiskey smells floated through the air. The women passed by men lining a thick slab of wood slung across two oak barrels that served as a bar. Other men sat on boxes surrounding tables made of barrels, drinking rotgut whiskey out of black bottles and clinking glasses. The intermingling of dozens of male voices created a heavy drone of sound.

Margarita scrutinized the population carefully. She sought a certain face: a man who looked down on his luck, one who might be willing to work steady — one who looked hungry. She saw him toward the back of the room. "Come on," she said to Julia, who followed obediently.

It was hard to tell how old he was. His beard and hair were snow white, but his eyes displayed no sign of age. He looked haunted and destitute. In one shaking hand he held a glass of whiskey, in the other, a nearly empty bottle. He tossed his drink down quickly and without pause, poured himself another. He paid no heed to the women who stood before him.

"You need work?" Margarita asked.

The miner squinted at her through piercing blue eyes, giving no indication that he had understood.

"Never mind," she said and turned away.

Like a flash of lightning, the man reached up and grabbed her, locking her arm in a vise-like grip. "I'll work," he said. "Pay for my whiskey."

"Come now," she ordered. Meekly he dropped his hand from her and rose to follow his new employers. Margarita tossed a spinning gold piece to the barkeep. He snatched it from the air and smiled at her efficiency.

Outside the saloon, the man said, "I don't come cheap."

"I'll work your ass off so you don't," Julia warned. "You step out of line once and I'll throw you to the dogs."

Margarita looked at Julia with admiration.

"You'll bring firewood," Julia ordered. "All you can gather. All day long if you have to. You'll find good pasture for the stock. You'll sleep during the late afternoon and evenings. At night, you'll guard the tent and the stock. If you get drunk, if anything goes wrong, if anything is missing, you'll be shot."

"By who?" he gruffly asked.

"By me," Margarita told him, and drew her gun out of a deep pocket in her skirt. She popped off a single shot at a bottle lying alongside a tent and shattered it to smithereens.

Beneath his beard the man paled visibly. "Look, ladies, I don't know if —"

"I paid for your whiskey, mister," Margarita reminded him. "That was the agreement. You're working now. Come back in an hour with wood and I'll feed you."

Without another word the man walked a bit unsteadily toward the hills and canyons that surrounded Dimmick's Goldfield.

"He'll either come back or he won't," Julia announced.

"Let's see what we can do about baking at least one cake," Margarita suggested. "If we can give him one cake, he's ours."

At camp again, Margarita began at once to gather ingredients needed while Julia went to search out where the chickens were laying and to milk the cow staked in a grassy area nearby.

"We'll have to move old Bossy this evening," Julia advised upon returning with a white foaming bucket and a half dozen eggs cradled carefully within her apron.

"I'm glad of that," Margarita answered. "I don't want a cow living right outside my tent. Draws flies."

She had gathered enough wood to get a fire going in the oven and had only been waiting for Julia to return with the milk and eggs. She went busily about her tasks as she and Julia talked. In another five minutes the batter was poured into two circular tins, struck sharply against the oven top to knock out air bubbles, and placed in the hot oven.

While they worked, their new helper brought a stack of deadwood. He did not speak but went efficiently about his duties. When the cake came out of the oven, he watched Julia place it on a cooling rack. "How long?" he grunted.

"An hour to cool, five minutes to frost," she answered.

"Chocolate frostin'?"

"Yes."

The man sauntered off wordlessly, returning several more times with wood that he was scrounging up from where the women could not imagine. The place was stripped practically bare now.

* * * * *

In a week's time, the bakers and the dancehall girl had settled solidly into a routine. Their handyman and guard, Jacob — a name he did not reveal until after he had totally consumed the chocolate cake Margarita had baked for him — was turning out to be highly efficient. After a couple of days and numerous curses, he had reassembled the wagon, using it to fetch all the firewood 'my ladies' needed, which was how he referred to the women who kept him well fed and spoke to him like he was a man again.

"I told you a cake would make him ours," Margarita gloated.

The oven was used daily from first light until early evening. The novelty of baking outdoors had still not worn off; the women were glad of the fresh air even when the weather was blistering hot, which it had been five days out of the seven they had been here. Only once had it rained, and Julia and Margarita had slept the day away.

They put in long, tiring hours, but before the sun sank from the sky they sold everything they had made that day. They were now sure their gamble on coming here had been smart and would pay off handsomely.

They were sure that Belle, too, must be stacking up a sizable sum. She was as busy throughout the night as her friends were during the day. Margarita and Julia asked each other more than once how Belle managed to sleep during the day with all the noise going on. But it didn't seem to affect her, and she kept her own hours, complete with time for a bath and three square meals a day. "I know the value of taking good care of myself," she told them one evening. "But it's tough. I'm going to look around for something to sink my money into after I get out of this racket."

"Like what?" Julia has asked.

"Oil, maybe. Or those electric glass bulb things you talked about last summer, Julia. Electricity could replace lanterns, you know."

Her friends laughed and said, "It'll never happen. You might better invest in oil. We'll be needing the kerosene for lanterns — lights that will endure forever."

Days passed into weeks. Miners, their mouths watering, came hungry to the bakers' camp, and left with a fifteen dollar pie in their hands, or a twenty dollar cake, or a fistful of cookies at two dollars each. Gold dust was the most frequent mode of payment. A teaspoonful was worth sixteen dollars, a wineglassful, one hundred dollars, and a tumbler, a thousand.

On their second day in camp, Julia had purchased a small set of scales from the hardware store, the dwelling nothing more than a rickety one-story building crammed full of picks, shovels, hammers, pans, denim pants, flannel shirts, hats, heavy leather boots, guns, bullets, lanterns, oil, scales, and anything else a miner might need that he had failed to bring with him — all at astronomical prices.

The nights became colder and the days shorter, and Margarita became more and more restless as summer drew to a close. Soon it would be time to tell Julia of her plans to leave. Living with her lovely Americano had been a joy and full of adventure, lovemaking had been rich and wonderful, and uncomfortable on the narrow cots with neither daring make a sound no matter how much she may have wanted to. And always, Julia has sworn her love, never once making a demand on Margarita to swear hers in return. Never even suggesting that she should do so.

But their life together was nearly over. Margarita had never been able to reconcile herself to her relationship with Julia. Something was missing and she had spent months trying to put her finger on whatever it was that was disturbing her. She had not been able to. It wasn't enough that Julia loved her, wanted them to spend their lives together. Whatever it was that was troubling her, she must discover it alone.

She broached the subject tentatively one evening after they had gone to bed and lay in their cots in the golden light of the lantern. Julia looked tired and drawn from too many hours at the oven, yet happiness radiated from her face. Margarita could feel her heart begin to beat faster as she realized just how nervous she was and how difficult this was going to be.

"I've sent money to my mother through the summer," she began. "But now I have enough dust to take to her so that she would be comfortable for a long time. I should go there soon; change the dust to bills and see how everyone is."

"That would be wonderful," Julia responded. "How long would you stay?"

"I might stay a very long time," Margarita replied.

Julia spoke too quickly. "A long time? Why a long time? We'll finally have enough to begin what we planned. We should get started soon. You don't need to be gone long."

Margarita sensed that Julia knew what was on her mind. She hadn't the heart or the courage to go on, and let conversation die there. When the time came, Margarita knew with certainty, her going would be very hard on Julia.

She had hoped that Julia might take an interest in her long time friend, Belle, or in one of the many flattering men who dropped by, the rewards they offered, their promises of a better life. Of the three of them, Julia seemed the least affected by their praise. If Margarita had been ready to marry, she might have seriously considered someone's offer.

She decided that she must set a date to finally act. It was the only way she was ever going to get through this. In a week's time she promised herself. One week from today she would tell Julia, and make her understand.

Chapter Nineteen

One of the saloons burned to the ground taking with it the flophouse to its left, and the general kitchen — and its cook — to the right. Everyone thanked whatever deity they followed that more damage had not been done and then cursed the drunken sot who had shot out one of the saloon's lanterns which had burst and spread flames everywhere. Then they had promptly dragged the kicking, screaming culprit to the nearest tree and hanged him.

Margarita hated with all her heart and soul what the camp had done, but the place had its own set of rules and they were swift and merciless. Loathing their heinous act, wanting to leave Dimmick's as soon as possible, she had still volunteered to work, along with the rest of the women in Dimmick's, in the temporary kitchen that had been thrown together to help feed the countless souls left without any kind of decent meal. She brought with her what plates, cups, and silverware that could be spared, and to that Belle added blankets. Others with extra supplies donated, too, and within a few hours of the fire, things were running fairly smooth again.

Salvaged from the kitchen's ruins, large black kettles three feet wide and two and a half feet deep hung over open fires giving off delicious aromas of boiling potatoes, carrots, cabbage, onions, and seasonings — ingredients that had wisely been stored in an outbuilding away from the saloon fire. On spits, large carcasses of beef rotated.

Finally the dancehall girls, who Margarita had begun supervising for the past week, learned from her how to keep the men alive without destroying their palates, and took over the chores completely. She wouldn't be back to help them tomorrow and she was grateful. Baking was an orderly business. Cooking for hordes was riotous and confusing, each man having to eat as quickly as possible so that another could take his seat, and use his plate and cup.

She returned to the tent late in the afternoon, her mind on what she must, at last, do, glad and frightened at the same time that it was almost over.

On the way back, she recalled the good times that she and Julia had shared here. How carefully they had, throughout the summer, weighed their precious dust each evening by lantern light. Using their little scales, they had meticulously measured to the grain, then poured equal amounts into every sack. The assayer himself wouldn't have been able to tell without his big fine scales any difference between the bags, each no bigger than a fist. And they hadn't actually cared which one weighed the most. It was just a game with them; a child's silly desire to see things divided perfectly even. It was fun to stack the gold on the table with the gentle yellow of the lantern's glow casting playful shadows across the small bags.

Her mind moved to thoughts of laughing with Julia as miners told outrageous stories of what had happened to them at their claims. She had difficulty thinking at all about the many nights Julia had spent running her strong firm hands across her body. Margarita blinked those memories away, too pleasant and too painful to recall.

Julia had just finished chores when Margarita arrived. I thought you'd never get here. Look." Julia pulled from her pocket a nugget as big as her fist. It was nearly pure. "That'll buy you six horses and me a hundred tubes of paint."

"Julia . . ." Margarita began.

"Heft it," Julia offered.

Margarita did not raise her hand. "Julia," she began again.

Julia dropped the nugget into an apron pocket, weighing the apron down ridiculously, and looked at Margarita with eyes tinged with fear. "It's come, hasn't it?"

"We need to talk. Please can't we go somewhere?"

Julia stared at her for some time before saying, "No. I don't think we need to go anywhere. I know what's on your mind. It's been there since I don't know when."

Margarita felt her face begin to burn as embarrassment and shame threatened to engulf her. She didn't want the end to be like this.

"Oh, I knew it was just a matter of time, Margarita. You're going to tell me that you're leaving me. Let's not drag this out. Just tell me when."

Julia's hands began to fidget, the way they had that day so long ago when a bandito had sat high in the saddle staring down on her, wanting to hate her, and unable to do so. Margarita could feel herself caving in.

"When will you be leaving?" Julia asked again.

The chill in her voice saved Margarita from herself. Quickly she answered, "As soon as I can. I need to buy a couple of horses and a saddle."

"Then I might as well return to Colter. I can't do this alone. We agreed to sell this stuff when we were finished here, right?" She encompassed the area with a careless flip of her hand. "I'd say that we're finished."

"You can keep the money from it."

"No, fair is fair." She was already embittered; her voice was thick with the sound. "I'll keep what the oven will sell for. The rest we'll split."

She walked away, giving Margarita no chance for further comment.

And what could she have added?

Julia was cold and distant for the three days it took Margarita to purchase all that she needed for the ride to Mexico. During that time, the gold was divided, the business as well as the tent itself sold and the proceeds divided; and from them both, the amount of dust it would take to pay back Colter Bank was converted to dollars and entrusted to Julia's care.

Belle was so disappointed the night before Margarita's departure that she could barely listen to Margarita's farewell. "Hell, woman, stay. You're making good money and for damn sure you're never gonna find a better friend

214

than Julia. You know damn well you mean all the world to her."

All the world to Julia? It was too heavy a load for Margarita to bear, and she only replied, "I've got what I came here for. Julia will be fine."

"Shit," was Belle's answer. She turned her back on Margarita and would not speak to her again.

Early on the fourth morning, Margarita donned men's clothing, strapped a gun on her hip, checked her pack horse once more to be sure her nineteen thousand dollars in paper money was deep and secure in a pack.

Julia had not stirred in her cot while Margarita gathered her things together, but as Margarita was about to mount up, she emerged from the tent, a nightrobe pulled tightly about her. Her hair was tousled, her eyes squinting against the early morning light.

"I can't just let you ride off, Margarita. I tried. I just couldn't do it."

"I'm sorry, Julia. I never meant to hurt you."

"I should have listened harder, I guess. I just thought . . . that after a time . . . if enough time went by. . . ."

"I'm sorry," Margarita repeated again. She longed to be off, away from this painful parting.

Julia gave Margarita a warm hug. Margarita didn't mean to be stiff about it, but was afraid of crying, of hanging on. She only barely returned Julia's embrace before breaking away.

Quickly she mounted up, muttering some meaningless thing to fill in the gaping silence, then nudged her mount's sides, dragging the packhorse behind.

"Write sometime, Margarita," Julia called after her.

"I will," Margarita lied.

Five or six miles went by before she could stop taking the continuous deep breaths necessary to fight the tears and sobs threatening to overwhelm her.

Chapter Twenty

With winter only weeks away, Margarita had no desire to cope with raising horses through the difficult coming months even though now as the best time to purchase stock. She didn't believe she could handle the responsibility. She didn't think she was capable of anything for a while except seeing to her family and just letting the rest of the world go straight to hell.

Two weeks later she found that she had had enough of Mexico. A thousand times she had answered her mother's worried questions: Why did she ride the country alone?

How had she been treated at the mining town? Why had she not yet found someone who might take Seth's place? The children got on her nerves with their demanding presence, wanting her to play with them, to look at every new little thing they discovered, to take them for walks. She had looked forward to coming. Now she looked forward to leaving.

A few days later she did so. She remembered that whenever she had been left alone at the meadow she had been happy. It was there that she would go. Her family watched her ride away, her mother's eyes full of tears and worry, her brothers and sisters in awe of their older sister, that she lived as she did.

She traveled by day, staying always alert in the open and unknown country. She checked her pistol frequently, making sure that it hadn't snuggled itself firmly into its holster, slowing her efforts to yank it out quickly should the need arise.

She was nervous and jumpy, afraid of the Indians she occasionally saw watching her from some distant bluff or hill. Why they didn't chase her, she had no idea. She could only pray that they would not.

She swung by Loma Parda, buying three extra packhorses, and a winter's supply of grain, food, blankets, and clothing.

It was a little more than six weeks before she finally reached the creek bed of the trail leading to the old hideaway. She was relieved to be there and could hardly wait to get to the meadow.

Old habits and instincts returned as she stealthily rode the trail up through the canyon. Familiar smells and sounds assaulted her, and she felt a wave of nostalgia hit her as she neared the gate.

She didn't know what to expect. Maybe Sam had returned from Mexico. For one fleeting moment she had the insane hope that Julia might even be here waiting for her.

She dismounted to move the gate aside, drawing the animals through before resetting the barrier and mounting again. "This part of the meadow hasn't changed," she said. Her breath billowed out before her in a white smoky cloud. It would not be long before the snows came.

From where she was, she could see the buildings were still the same. A little tired looking, but not much different otherwise. And Sam had not come back. She was completely alone.

She drew up before her old dwelling and dismounted, glad to be out of the saddle. She unloaded the supplies and turned the horses loose, slapping their hides, forcing them away from the cabin. They trotted a few feet away and began to nibble on crunchy grass.

She went inside and began to put her things away with only the sounds of her own rustlings and comments she idly made aloud to keep herself company.

There was plenty of firewood in the shed, cut and stacked by the men over a year ago, and each evening Margarita would haul enough wood inside to keep the fire going twenty-four hours a day.

Night and day she fought turbulent emotions, driving them deeper and deeper into the darkest recesses of her mind, not allowing herself to ponder what tormented her. Instead she considered when she might marry. She would build a new life with her husband, raise horses, own some of the best range in New Mexico. She had the money. She could do it very successfully. She had everything she wanted now. She was long since free of the dark side of

219

the law. Every peso she owned had been honestly earned, a bright outlook for the future.

One cold brisk morning, after an unusually sleepless night, she cursed loudly into the cistern's reflection of herself. "You stupid little fool, why do you do this to yourself?"

With this statement, new questions began to surface. She began to wonder at having left Julia. Sometimes she almost hated the woman for having made her so dependent upon her. Margarita didn't know how it had happened. She had been so careful not to let it; she laughed bitterly at herself because it had.

Had some damn woman really stolen her heart and soul after all? It was an honest question, and it made her cry.

She began to play a game with herself, one that kept her mind occupied when she was the most tired, when she couldn't sleep. She would recall each and every time Julia had ever said "I love you." She counted up the times and played with the figures at which she had arrived. In detail, she would attempt to relive every situation they had ever been in when Julia had whispered or spoken the beautiful words; the tone of her voice, the look on her face. Margarita often felt flames of shame sear her cheeks because she had never once said the same to Julia. Even if she hadn't understood that she loved her, she could have lied on the outside chance that she had been wrong.

But she hadn't given an inch. Not one inch.

By the end of February, twenty-foot drifts banked the trail's opening to the valley below, completely sealing off the meadow and trapping Margarita until spring. She kept a roaring blaze going in the fireplace during the day and let the wood burn down at night to a comfortable glowing bed of coals.

She had plenty of fuel for the lanterns, so there was no need to go to bed early. But there was no reason to stay up. She had no books to read, there was no one to talk to. And so even before the final light of day had died she was in bed and asleep.

During her waking hours, she thought of Julia until she wanted to scream and tear her hair. She had made her decision at Dimmick's Goldfield: a life with Julia was an impossibility. She had spent hours envisioning what it might be like living with her. She could find no flaws in the partnership, no major obstacles. It was just that she could not identify with such a kinship.

So she came to a final and absolute decision here at the meadow, aware that the debate raged within her still. She would never see Julia again. She would no longer toy with the idea of a life with her, and refused to think further about her at all.

To succeed at this discipline, she did everything she could to keep busy. Several times she climbed onto the roofs of both cabins and the shed to clear them of snow. She brushed the horses' thick coats daily and kept their shelter clean enough to live in. She fashioned snowshoes out of thin green pine branches laced together with thongs. The shoes were poorly made but she managed to get around on them, daily forcing herself to walk the perimeter of the meadow. On clear days she would stand near its edge and gaze at the valley far below.

It was early June before enough snow had melted off so that she could leave. She had spent the winter planning exactly what she would do, and at first opportunity strung the horses, saddled her own, and led them all down the trail and away from her self-imposed prison.

221

She glanced over her shoulder for one final time at the meadow, still and quiet now and devoid of life as it waited for the last of its lingering snow patches to disappear. Soon small birds and butterflies and buzzing insects would return to a thick grassy surface and brilliantly colored flowers.

She thought she, too, might return one day. The place was hers now. She had staked a legal claim to it, building cairns at various points to identify the boundaries. She had included the entire meadow and the pool above. Without acknowledging her own motives, she had set the place up as a living monument to what she and Julia had once shared.

When she reached the stream below, the main canyon was raging with spring runoff. For a moment she wondered if she should attempt to go any further. When she hit the creek bed, it would be bad. But to turn back seemed impossible now that she had left, and so, winding the lead packhorse's rope tightly around the saddle horn, she gently kicked her mount in the flanks and continued her journey.

She had her money and enough food to sustain her until she reached Lincoln County where she would begin her new farm and raise quality horses for the army. She had had at least enough stamina not to let that dream slip away, although she didn't seem to have the same heart for it that she once had.

She dismounted and checked each animal, talking to them all, patting them firmly on the neck and scratching their ears, trying to reassure and calm them. She mounted up again and said, "All right, you haybags, let's go," and led the skittish, prancing animals slowly into the bitingly cold stream.

The water sucked and dragged at the reluctant horses' hooves and legs, causing them to pull against the lead rope, but Margarita shouted words of encouragement over her shoulder to them. Their ears flicked back and forth, the horses nervously listening to her voice and the gushing water flowing around them.

It took a half hour to get out of the energy-sapping stream. Margarita rode a short distance away before stopping to check the supplies again. Everything was still in good order. The only thing now was to head south.

She would make only twenty miles today. It was the first time the horses had traveled since late last fall and she didn't want to tire them unnecessarily; nor herself either, for that matter. She had a lot of time. All the time in the world.

She glanced northeast, the direction that Colter lay, then wondered why she did. It was just a place now. A town she had once spent some time in.

She breathed a deep, melancholy sigh, unable to make herself go forward. An overwhelming sense of despair filled her and she had to fight to refrain from crying. She leaned over her saddle horn, her hands supporting her, her head down as she fought for control.

I'm leaving the meadow, she thought. And I've already left Colter — forever. She would never see Julia again.

The words nearly crushed the life from her.

Chapter Twenty-One

Five days after she had left the creekbed, she was still reminding herself that it wouldn't hurt a thing to stop at Colter and say hello to Julia. That she herself had personal effects at the house, left behind last spring. Nothing worth picking up, but it was a legitimate excuse for being there.

As she drew abreast of the building, her heart began to pound. It was as though the past year had never occurred; a blink of an eye in time, the space of a single breath.

She recognized small things about the place she had not consciously paid any attention to when she had lived there. That loose board on the barn next to the door that still needed to be repaired, the one picket missing from the fence that extended across the front yard. Nothing had changed at all. Margarita felt the house's presence as a living thing, reopening a raw wound, stinging and exhausting her.

It had been a terrible mistake to come here.

As she drew up to the fence, she noticed a small sign hanging on its gate. An awful wave of disappointment struck her as she read the name: MEREDITH. Julia, married? She didn't want Julia to be married. She wanted Julia to remain single, unspoiled by a man.

She wanted Julia for herself.

Only when she read the name, did she know. It had taken her until this moment to learn what had kept her from giving herself completely to Julia: that age-old adage that women must marry; *she* must marry. Who had beaten that idea into her brain, searing it there? Why was the thought so ridiculously universal an expectation that it left no room for anything else? She had gotten so caught up in ancient customs and ironclad standards that she had been blinded to all else. Julia had never been. Julia had been in love with her. That was all Julia had ever needed to know. Julia had never fought with herself over it. Julia had just accepted it, not trying to understand nor to philosophize over it, nor worry over what the rest of the world did.

But because she had doubts and concerns and had stayed locked up in her own little world, Margarita was now on the outside of this house, and the married Julia Meredith was inside. Her heart cried out over her greatest misdeed.

225

Then she thought: Perhaps it's a tenant's name. Hope filled her heart. She rode up to the fence and dismounted.

With deliberate motions, she draped the reins carefully over the fence. Opening the gate, she stepped into the yard. She felt dreamlike, felt as if she were walking through thick molasses that dragged mercilessly at her every step, her every movement, impairing her breathing and clouding her vision.

Tentatively and timidly, she stepped onto the porch, then knocked on the door.

The door opened wide. "Margarita," Julia gasped. She stood silent after that, trying to form words, but none came.

Margarita felt a shaft of pain pierce her breast. She had been wrong. There was no tenant.

Julia looked pale and wan. She was very thin. Gone was the rosy-appled look in her cheeks and the spark in her blue eyes. Even her yellow hair had dulled a bit.

"I was in the area." Margarita spoke lightly. She would not want Julia to think she wasn't happy for her.

Julia stepped back. "Come in. I'm so glad to see you. You look . . . good."

She looked like hell from months of living alone and days on the trail, and she knew it. But Julia had always been kind to her.

"I hope I'm not interrupting anything."

"No, come in. I'm in the kitchen."

Margarita wanted to sweep Julia against her breast, to hold her, kiss her. She kept her hands busy by tightly clutching her hat so that she would not do something foolish.

"I see you're a Meredith, now. My congratulations to you."

Julia smiled a tight little smile.

226

Margarita wanted to ask when it was that Julia had married. Right after she got back? Had she missed Margarita that much? Or had it been a long romantic engagement?

Oh,, Lord, why didn't Julia reach for her? Just for old time's sake?

"I'll make you something to drink," Julia said formally.

Margarita followed her into the kitchen.

A new cookstove sat where the old one had been. On the table were piles of a man's and a woman's clothing. It was difficult to accept seeing a man's clothing touching Julia's own. And there, too, sat a small crib on the floor beside the table.

"A cradle?" Margarita asked. She stared at it, her head just a little dizzy.

"My own when I was an infant," Julia explained. She placed a fond hand on it and gave it a little push. It rocked slowly back and forth. "Soon, another will sleep in it."

Margarita could not bring herself to ask when Julia was due. She sat sipping warm lemonade while Julia folded fresh laundry taken from the back line, giving each piece a sharp whack before folding it neatly and setting it aside. She talked very little about what she was doing these days, about what she had done after she had returned to Colter from Dimmick's. Belle had come back with her and now owned a majority interest in the Low Dog Saloon. She mentioned that when she had paid their loan back, Marsh had just about had apoplexy when she returned the full amount in a lump sum. Maude still ran the drugstore and was running it into the ground, from all reports. It was obvious that Julia did not want to discuss herself. The days of their close intimacy were over.

With nothing left to say — nothing that she *could* say — Margarita uttered, "I must go now, Julia. . . ." Reluctantly she rose and thanked her for the drink. At the front door she paused, awkwardly turning the brim of her hat in her hands.

Julia had followed her but made no move toward her.

"I wish you well, Margarita. Will you raise those horses you talked about?"

"I suppose. And are you painting?"

"Not much."

Throwing a shawl over her shoulders, Julia followed Margarita to the waiting horses. Margarita stood looking up at the taller Julia. When she rode away this time, she would never return. She would be unable to. "Goodbye, Julia." Gracefully she swung into the saddle.

"Goodbye, Margarita."

She glanced at Julia just one more time. The blue in her eyes was more than Margarita could endure. She clucked to her horse and turned her face away.

"Margarita," Julia called after her.

Margarita ignored her, keeping the horse at a steady walk, pulling the packhorses with her. From long ago, the echo of Sam's words came back to her: "You got too much honor, Margarita. It's gonna cost you someday." She would only get into terrible trouble if she turned, and she would not act honorably at all. She would grab Julia to her this time. And that would be a disgraceful act.

Julia called again as Margarita rode further and further away.

"I will never marry, Margarita. Never!"

Never marry? Julia wasn't married? But the sign on the fence. . . . She had even said she was.

Margarita reined up and brought her mount around, stunned and blinking, thinking that if she had heard wrong, she would not be able to live.

She dropped the packhorses' rope and rode back to Julia's side. "But the clothes, the men's clothes, the baby's crib. You *said* you were."

"You assumed I was. Meredith's not my name, Margarita. It belongs to the people who rent this place." Julia began to cry, and then to sob. "Herb Elkins' family . . . over on the river, they lost everything they own in a fire last night. I'm here only long enough to collect clothing and the crib for their baby. I don't live here, Margarita. I will *never* marry, I tell you." Her fists were clenched tightly at her side, and her voice cracked as she spoke. "Oh, damn it, Margarita, I have no pride. *None!*"

"Julia." Margarita was out of the saddle in an instant. She grabbed Julia by both arms. "But you never made a move toward me at the door, a gesture, a hug. You did not deny you were married."

"I didn't dare. You looked so strong, so aloof — as if you still didn't need me. You and your damnable unbendable strength."

"But I do need you. I've always needed you. But. . . ." But why explain the stupidity and blindness of one's soul to the seeing?

Julia slipped her arms around the smaller woman and held her as closely as Margarita held her. Their tears mingled as they cried and kissed silently.

"Dear Margarita," Julia said. "Dear, dear little Yellowthroat. My life was over without you."

Margarita sobbed through gushing tears she tried to brush aside. At last able to speak, she said, "I will tell you

229

now, Julia Blake, that I love you. I have for a long, long time. How terribly blind I was — have always been. I will never leave you. I swear to you."

Julia smiled but did not reply with similar words.

Margarita did not need to hear Julia make the same vow. It had always existed for Julia. Only Margarita had been the thick-witted one.

She tucked her head comfortingly beneath Julia's chin, just as she used to. They stood together in the long afternoon rays of a warm yellow sun, arms strongly encircling one another.

A few of the publications of
THE NAIAD PRESS, INC.
P.O. Box 10543 • Tallahassee, Florida 32302
Phone (904) 539-9322
Mail orders welcome. Please include 15% postage.

YELLOWTHROAT by Penny Hayes. 240 pp. Margarita, bandit, kidnaps Julia. ISBN 0-941483-10-X — $8.95

LESSONS IN MURDER by Claire McNab. 216 pp. 1st in a stylish mystery series. ISBN 0-941483-14-2 — 8.95

CHERISHED LOVE by Evelyn Kennedy. 192 pp. Erotic Lesbian love story. ISBN 0-941483-08-8 — 8.95

LAST SEPTEMBER by Helen R. Hull. 208 pp. Six stories & a glorious novella. ISBN 0-941483-09-6 — 8.95

THE SECRET IN THE BIRD by Camarin Grae. 312 pp. Striking, psychological suspense novel. ISBN 0-941483-05-3 — 8.95

TO THE LIGHTNING by Catherine Ennis. 208 pp. Romantic Lesbian 'Robinson Crusoe' adventure. ISBN 0-941483-06-1 — 8.95

THE OTHER SIDE OF VENUS by Shirley Verel. 224 pp. Luminous, romantic love story. ISBN 0-941483-07-X — 8.95

DREAMS AND SWORDS by Katherine V. Forrest. 192 pp. Romantic, erotic, imaginative stories. ISBN 0-941483-03-7 — 8.95

MEMORY BOARD by Jane Rule. 336 pp. Memorable novel about an aging Lesbian couple. ISBN 0-941483-02-9 — 8.95

THE ALWAYS ANONYMOUS BEAST by Lauren Wright Douglas. 224 pp. A Caitlin Reese mystery. First in a series. ISBN 0-941483-04-5 — 8.95

SEARCHING FOR SPRING by Patricia A. Murphy. 224 pp. Novel about the recovery of love. ISBN 0-941483-00-2 — 8.95

DUSTY'S QUEEN OF HEARTS DINER by Lee Lynch. 240 pp. Romantic blue-collar novel. ISBN 0-941483-01-0 — 8.95

PARENTS MATTER by Ann Muller. 240 pp. Parents' relationships with Lesbian daughters and gay sons. ISBN 0-930044-91-6 — 9.95

THE PEARLS by Shelley Smith. 176 pp. Passion and fun in the Caribbean sun. ISBN 0-930044-93-2 — 7.95

MAGDALENA by Sarah Aldridge. 352 pp. Epic Lesbian novel set on three continents. ISBN 0-930044-99-1 — 8.95

THE BLACK AND WHITE OF IT by Ann Allen Shockley. 144 pp. Short stories. ISBN 0-930044-96-7 — 7.95

SAY JESUS AND COME TO ME by Ann Allen Shockley. 288 pp. Contemporary romance. ISBN 0-930044-98-3   8.95

LOVING HER by Ann Allen Shockley. 192 pp. Romantic love story. ISBN 0-930044-97-5   7.95

MURDER AT THE NIGHTWOOD BAR by Katherine V. Forrest. 240 pp. A Kate Delafield mystery. Second in a series. ISBN 0-930044-92-4   8.95

ZOE'S BOOK by Gail Pass. 224 pp. Passionate, obsessive love story. ISBN 0-930044-95-9   7.95

WINGED DANCER by Camarin Grae. 228 pp. Erotic Lesbian adventure story. ISBN 0-930044-88-6   8.95

PAZ by Camarin Grae. 336 pp. Romantic Lesbian adventurer with the power to change the world. ISBN 0-930044-89-4   8.95

SOUL SNATCHER by Camarin Grae. 224 pp. A puzzle, an adventure, a mystery — Lesbian romance. ISBN 0-930044-90-8   8.95

THE LOVE OF GOOD WOMEN by Isabel Miller. 224 pp. Long-awaited new novel by the author of the beloved *Patience and Sarah.* ISBN 0-930044-81-9   8.95

THE HOUSE AT PELHAM FALLS by Brenda Weathers. 240 pp. Suspenseful Lesbian ghost story. ISBN 0-930044-79-7   7.95

HOME IN YOUR HANDS by Lee Lynch. 240 pp. More stories from the author of *Old Dyke Tales.* ISBN 0-930044-80-0   7.95

EACH HAND A MAP by Anita Skeen. 112 pp. Real-life poems that touch us all. ISBN 0-930044-82-7   6.95

SURPLUS by Sylvia Stevenson. 342 pp. A classic early Lesbian novel. ISBN 0-930044-78-9   6.95

PEMBROKE PARK by Michelle Martin. 256 pp. Derring-do and daring romance in Regency England. ISBN 0-930044-77-0   7.95

THE LONG TRAIL by Penny Hayes. 248 pp. Vivid adventures of two women in love in the old west. ISBN 0-930044-76-2   8.95

HORIZON OF THE HEART by Shelley Smith. 192 pp. Hot romance in summertime New England. ISBN 0-930044-75-4   7.95

AN EMERGENCE OF GREEN by Katherine V. Forrest. 288 pp. Powerful novel of sexual discovery. ISBN 0-930044-69-X   8.95

THE LESBIAN PERIODICALS INDEX edited by Claire Potter. 432 pp. Author & subject index. ISBN 0-930044-74-6   29.95

DESERT OF THE HEART by Jane Rule. 224 pp. A classic; basis for the movie *Desert Hearts.* ISBN 0-930044-73-8   7.95

SPRING FORWARD/FALL BACK by Sheila Ortiz Taylor. 288 pp. Literary novel of timeless love. ISBN 0-930044-70-3   7.95

FOR KEEPS by Elisabeth Nonas. 144 pp. Contemporary novel about losing and finding love. ISBN 0-930044-71-1   7.95

BLACK LESBIAN IN WHITE AMERICA by Anita Cornwell.
141 pp. Stories, essays, autobiography.   ISBN 0-930044-41-X   7.50

CONTRACT WITH THE WORLD by Jane Rule. 340 pp.
Powerful, panoramic novel of gay life.   ISBN 0-930044-28-2   7.95

YANTRAS OF WOMANLOVE by Tee A. Corinne. 64 pp.
Photos by noted Lesbian photographer.   ISBN 0-930044-30-4   6.95

MRS. PORTER'S LETTER by Vicki P. McConnell. 224 pp.
The first Nyla Wade mystery.   ISBN 0-930044-29-0   7.95

TO THE CLEVELAND STATION by Carol Anne Douglas.
192 pp. Interracial Lesbian love story.   ISBN 0-930044-27-4   6.95

THE NESTING PLACE by Sarah Aldridge. 224 pp. A
three-woman triangle—love conquers all!   ISBN 0-930044-26-6   7.95

THIS IS NOT FOR YOU by Jane Rule. 284 pp. A letter to a
beloved is also an intricate novel.   ISBN 0-930044-25-8   8.95

FAULTLINE by Sheila Ortiz Taylor. 140 pp. Warm, funny,
literate story of a startling family.   ISBN 0-930044-24-X   6.95

THE LESBIAN IN LITERATURE by Barbara Grier. 3d ed.
Foreword by Maida Tilchen. 240 pp. Comprehensive bibliography.
Literary ratings; rare photos.   ISBN 0-930044-23-1   7.95

ANNA'S COUNTRY by Elizabeth Lang. 208 pp. A woman
finds her Lesbian identity.   ISBN 0-930044-19-3   6.95

PRISM by Valerie Taylor. 158 pp. A love affair between two
women in their sixties.   ISBN 0-930044-18-5   6.95

BLACK LESBIANS: AN ANNOTATED BIBLIOGRAPHY
compiled by J. R. Roberts. Foreword by Barbara Smith. 112 pp.
Award-winning bibliography.   ISBN 0-930044-21-5   5.95

THE MARQUISE AND THE NOVICE by Victoria Ramstetter.
108 pp. A Lesbian Gothic novel.   ISBN 0-930044-16-9   4.95

OUTLANDER by Jane Rule. 207 pp. Short stories and essays
by one of our finest writers.   ISBN 0-930044-17-7   6.95

SAPPHISTRY: THE BOOK OF LESBIAN SEXUALITY by
Pat Califia. 3d edition, revised. 208 pp.   ISBN 0-941483-24-X   8.95

ALL TRUE LOVERS by Sarah Aldridge. 292 pp. Romantic
novel set in the 1930s and 1940s.   ISBN 0-930044-10-X   7.95

A WOMAN APPEARED TO ME by Renee Vivien. 65 pp. A
classic; translated by Jeannette H. Foster.   ISBN 0-930044-06-1   5.00

CYTHEREA'S BREATH by Sarah Aldridge. 240 pp. Romantic
novel about women's entrance into medicine.
                                        ISBN 0-930044-02-9   6.95

TOTTIE by Sarah Aldridge. 181 pp. Lesbian romance in the
turmoil of the sixties.   ISBN 0-930044-01-0   6.95

THE LATECOMER by Sarah Aldridge. 107 pp. A delicate love
story.   ISBN 0-930044-00-2   5.00